ASSAULT ON THE ROCK

Recent Titles by Duncan Harding from Severn House

Writing as Duncan Harding

Clash in the Baltic
Convoy of Death
Hell on the Rhine
Massacre at Jutland
The Normandie Mission
Operation Judgement
Operation Torch
Ramps Down, Troops Away!
Sink the Ark Royal
Sink the Bismarck
Sink the Cossack
Sink the Prince of Wales
Sink the Warspite
Slaughter in Singapore
The Tobruk Rescue

Writing as Leo Kessler

S.S. Wotan Series

Assault On Baghdad
The Great Escape
Hitler Youth Attacks
Kill Patton
Operation Glenn Miller
Operation Iraq
Operation Leningrad
Patton's Wall
The Screaming Eagles
Sirens of Dunkirk
Stalag Assault
Wotan Missions

Battle for Hitler's Eagles' Nest
The Blackout Murders
The Churchill Papers
Murder at Colditz

ASSAULT ON
THE ROCK

Duncan Harding

severn House

This first world edition published in Great Britain 2006 by
SEVERN HOUSE PUBLISHERS LTD of
9–15 High Street, Sutton, Surrey SM1 1DF.
This first world edition published in the USA 2006 by
SEVERN HOUSE PUBLISHERS INC of
595 Madison Avenue, New York, N.Y. 10022.

British Library Cataloguing in Publication Data

Harding, Duncan, 1926-
   Assault on the Rock
   1.   World War, 1939-1945 - Secret service - Great Britain - Fiction
   2.   Suspense fiction
   I.   Title
   823.9'14 [F]

   ISBN-13: 978-0-7278-6409-3
   ISBN-10: 0-7278-6409-2

Typeset by Palimpsest Book Pr
Grangemouth, Stirlingshire, Sc
Printed and bound in Great Bri
MPG Books Ltd., Bodmin, Co

Duncan Harding is Perplexed

The big 'lounge' smelled of piss.
Old ladies' urine to be exact. Which wasn't surprising. The lounge was filled with them. Doddery old biddies lined the walls in the Parker Knolls.

It had been my publisher's fault, really. He'd read the Spaniard's letter and was full of it. 'Dunc,' (he always called me 'Dunc' when he thought I was going to make him money) 'I think we've got a winner, a real winner.' He'd signalled to the old waiter, who creaked over as if he were badly in need of oiling, and ordered another bottle of 'Mouton', the red plonk he likes – and in the 'Gay Hussar' restaurant the 'Mouton' doesn't come cheap. That's why the place is full of pinko politicians; they're the only ones who can afford it these days.

'I mean,' he'd waffled while the fusty old waiter had gone through the motions of cleaning off the dust and cobwebs (my guess is that they spray the stuff on before they serve it, but no matter), 'this looks like the real McCoy for you to hang one of your celebrated historical works on.'

I don't like the Mouton stuff, but I like those famous words, 'Celebrated historical works'. They usually mean a decent advance – well, decent by the publisher's standards. 'There's some chap in Spain telling us that we Brits attempted to do away with General Franco, the Spanish dictator, during the war and prepared to give us chapter and verse – for free!' He'd beamed, and thus we sent off for the second bottle of Rothschild's plonk.

As you well know, gentle reader, beneath this tough, cynical exterior, I'm really a decent bloke. 'Salt of the earth, straight as a die', some other publisher wrote about me only the other day (I have a vague feeling he owes me money), and I didn't want my publisher to fall flat on his face about this one. 'But who knows who General Franco is these days?' I asked.

He died thirty years ago tomorrow, November twentieth 1975,' he announced completely out of the blue, and beamed at me proudly as if it was all very important. Real one-upmanship stuff. 'But who remembers him?' I'd objected. 'I mean, most folk these days will remember when Jimi Hendrix snuffed it, but a Spanish dictator . . .' I'd shrugged and left the rest of the sentence unsaid.

Which was wise, some Labour big shot was coming in, all camelhair coat, make-up and dyed hair, and the staff were falling over backwards to make a fuss of him. They might not be Hungarians any more, despite the place's name, but they still could make enough racket in bastard Cockney to drown every other sound.

'Ah, you have a point, Dunc, but remember there *are* one million Brits living in Spain these days – all middle or old age. They'd be interested, and their dear ones.' (My publisher is given to such sentimental terms, especially when he's high on the Mouton). 'Sell to them alone and we're on a winner . . .'

I didn't have to wait long. The proprietress, H. B. Hawkins, SRN, came in her expensive, flowered silk dress, with the corset lines showing through, grandly dispensing room spray to left and right. By the time she was finished, the place smelled of lavender (she ought to change the name of her home to Lavender Field).

I swallowed the Polo mint – I'd had a pint in the local in order not to smell – as she advanced upon us, all smiles and hard, cash-register eyes. In the pub, in the open-hearted manner of simple Gloucester folk, they'd told me she was a 'bloody Welsho . . . watch her, mate, or she'll have yer wallet.' She gave one last spray and then, all expensive capped teeth, she advanced upon me again and said, 'The writer Duncan Harding, I presume.' She presumed correctly. I was the writer Duncan Harding, but no one had ever addressed me like that, as if I'd just won the Booker Prize and had been on telly in an evening suit that didn't fit, waffling about my great novel dealing with the love affair of two black lesbians in Outer Mongolia.

'Come on along then,' she said with a gay smile – God, those capped teeth could have blinded a man if he weren't careful. 'I'll take you to her Ladyship. Would you like to take the stair lift?' I declined and we mounted the stairs – Axminster carpet, naturally: at five hundred quid a week, the old biddy could afford it. She panted, and when she though I wasn't looking, tugged hastily at the back of her corset. 'She's a bit of a card, but of course your aristocracy are like that, Mr Harding,' she explained. 'You'll probably have interviewed a lot of them in your writing career.' I nodded, as if I were the *Times* court Correspondent-in-Chief.

A few moments later she knocked discreetly and a high-pitched, brittle voice said, 'Come in,' and if Lady X, née Tidmus-Mcleod was bedridden, it was clear from the authority in her voice that she still had all her marbles. There she was, very skinny, but still pretty in the manner of some old trouts, the eyes a bit red, but sharp, very sharp, not even trying to hide her cigarette, despite the notices everywhere proclaiming, 'Please refrain from smoking. We are a non-smoking house.'

'Your visitor,' the Prop said, ignoring the cigarette in the long ivory holder, 'the writer Duncan Harding.' The old trout looked at me like she might have done to some poor little skivvy coming for her first job in the 'big house', and said in that really high voice of hers, 'Never heard of him.' With a wave of her hand; she dismissed the Prop, saying, 'None of that bloody Nescafe of yours either. If I want a cup of coffee, it has to be properly filtered.'

Smiling bravely, the Prop fled, and even before she'd closed the door, the old lady snapped, 'Bloody Welsho, rip you off at a glance.' The modern phrase caught me by surprise, but most of what she had to say that afternoon did the same. 'Now', she said straight off, 'you want to know about the Catalans, is that it?' She frowned and then said, 'Suppose I ought to tell you what I know, before this bloody lot finally catches up with me – she swept her bony hand, covered in liver spots, at the commode, the spare bedpans, the table piled with the pills. She chuckled suddenly. It was a strange sound coming from such an old person, who was obviously dying. 'Or the bloody Welsho tosses me into the workhouse because I can no longer pay her exorbitant bloody bills.'

'Well, Cusi and his Catalan exiles came into my life in the second year of the war, when I was seventeen and Daddy and I were living in Scotland in disgrace. Late summer 1940.' She gave a little sigh, and her red eyes looked momentarily very far away. 'Seventeen, and the second year of the war,' she repeated. 'Magic,' I thought I heard her say. 'Sheer magic!' I thought I might have been mistaken; her voice was abruptly quite faint. Suddenly she looked hard at me, 'It was the summer when we were all betrayed, of course . . .'

BOOK ONE

Operation Felix

'*Meine Herren*. This is the plan. We will let General Franco's Spaniards make the main assault on the Rock. They have the men. They can have the honour. German soldiers' lives are too precious to be wasted on such bloody operations.

Thereafter we Germans will take charge naturally. The Mediterranean will become a German lake. We shall drive the damned English out of the Middle East once and for all. The war with that drunken sot Churchill will be over . . . But one word of warning, *meine Herren*. There will be treachery afoot in Spain. The English will see to that . . . *GENTLEMEN, DON'T TRUST ANYONE* . . .'

Adolf Hitler to his Generals, Berchtesgaden, Winter 1941

Author's Note

In 1939, an outraged British Foreign Secretary, Lord Halifax, declared that 'British diplomacy is never carried out by means of assassination.' Then, it seemed, at the outbreak of World War Two, there was an unwritten agreement between Allied and enemy leaders that they would not attempt to murder each other.

In fact, throughout the war they did so or attempted to do so. King Boris of Bulgaria was murdered on Hitler's orders. Admiral Darlan, Deputy Leader of Vichy France, and *Gruppenführer* Heydrich, virtual dictator of German-occupied Czechoslovakia, were similarly assassinated at British command. Attempts to do the same – they all failed – were carried out by the Germans against Churchill, Stalin and President Roosevelt. For his part, Hitler survived attempt after attempt until he shot himself, trapped in his Berlin bunker in 1945.

But there was one attempted assassination on a *neutral* leader, which, for obvious reasons, has never been publicized or officially recognized. It was the British plan to murder the Spanish dictator, General Franco. In 1941 he was about to throw in his lot with Adolf Hitler. In return for entering the war on the German side, he would be given back Gibraltar, which had been in the hands of the 'English Occupiers' for two centuries. The attempt narrowly failed, and as we know, the 'Rock' is still part of Britain to this day. The price paid, however, was high in the lives of the Spaniards concerned with the plot. But now that tale can be told, nearly three quarters of a century after the terrible events of that summer of 1941. *Assault on the Rock* is not a pretty tale, but in those days, gentle reader, there were not many pretty tales, were there?

Duncan Harding

BOOK ONE

Sink the *Deutschland*!

One

B arcelona was about finished.
Down in the *Ramblas*, the Communists were battling it out with the local Republicans. Cusi and the rest could hear the slow chatter of a Soviet Maxim, followed an instant later by the swifter angry *brr* of a more modern French Hotchkiss. Over in the direction of Gaudi's cathedral, flames were leaping higher and higher into the winter sky, and on both sides of the streets, the Cusi group could hear the screams and shrieks of the hungry, angry peasants from the country raping the city women.

Jordi, who still had religion, crossed himself and wailed, 'It's like the end of the world, Lieutenant! God, how can such things happen in Christian Spain?'

Cusi, who was intent on getting through to the docks before he and the rest of the Catalan seamen volunteers were discovered by the patrols, Communist and Republican, which were everywhere in the dying city, ignored the question. Instead he barked in their native Catalan: '*a la dreta . . . a l'estacio de trens!*'

Gripping their weapons in hands which were suddenly damp with sweat despite the freezing cold wind which blew down from the snow-capped Pyrenees, the desperate band pushed on through the still-smoking ruins of the night's raid by Franco's bombers. They knew their lives were at stake. The Russian Communists who held the docks would shoot them down like dogs if they discovered what their mission was. The Soviets wanted to get the Republicans' gold out of the Catalan capital before it fell to Franco's troops; they wanted no trouble out at sea.

To the south, the Franco artillery started up again. On the

3

horizon, the purple darkness changed to a soft glowing pink, which became an angry violet, followed seconds later by the banshee-like howl of heavy howitzer shells slamming into the city, rocking the buildings all around the little band like stage props caught in a sudden wind. Masonry started to slither to the ground in a stone avalanche. One of the men yelped with pain. Blood began to trickle down his right arm. Still, he caught himself in time and staggered on towards the docks. He, like the rest of the volunteers, knew the importance of their mission. If they didn't succeed, the 'Fritzes' would massacre their comrades in the beaten Catalan Army, retreating along the coast towards Port Bou and the safety of neutral France.

'*A la esquerra*,' Cusi commanded sharply, and instinctively raised the big Luger he carried. To his immediate front, a group of Soviets in their leather coats were grouped around a flickering fire, wolfing down looted, half-charred meat, the grease running down their unshaven chins. They were drunk, like the Russian 'volunteers' to the Republican cause usually were; they didn't seem to notice the howitzer shells falling all around. Besides, they had half a dozen half-naked women squatting in the rubble, hands tied behind their backs, shivering and blue in the biting cold. Cusi knew what the Russians were up to: as soon as they had filled their bellies and were drunk enough, they'd rape the women and then shoot them. They always did with their captives.

Jordi, the religious one, started to groan.

Cusi silenced him with a curt whisper. 'Enough. Unless you want a Red prick stuck up your arse.'

The words were crude but effective. The moans died on Jordi's lips instantly. They pushed on.

Now, despite the acrid smoke and stink of gunpowder, they started to smell the oily tang of the sea. They were approaching the port.

Like grey, predatory timber wolves, their outlines silhouetted against the walls of the docks by the flames, they slipped one by one towards the quaysides. At regular intervals, the Soviets guarding the ships anchored there shot flares into the night sky. At such moments, they froze immediately. Their

4

hearts beat frantically. They could feel the cold beads of sweat trickling unpleasantly down the smalls of their backs. For what seemed an eternity, they dared not even breathe, until the flares tumbled to earth like fallen angels and extinguished. Then Cusi would hiss, 'On, comrades. There is no time to be wasted. The Reds are on their guard.'

They knew the ex-officer of the Republican Navy was right. It could be only a matter of hours now before the Russians would set sail, taking the *Banco de Espana*'s gold and the rest of their loot with them. Now the commissars who commanded the Russian 'volunteers' would be at the highest state of alert; they knew what Franco's victorious Moors would do to them once they entered a conquered Barcelona. It would be the firing squad for them – if they were lucky; castration and cruxification if they weren't.

Angles Cusi*, as his fellow midshipmen had once called him due to his blond hair and pale, Anglo-Saxon features, which he had inherited from his English mother, was not concerned with the fate of the Communists who had taken over the control of his native Barcelona in these last terrible months. His mind was on his mission. 'The last one, my dear *Teniente*,' as the defeated General Cugat had said, somewhat sadly, at the beginning of his briefing.

In essence, as General Cugat had explained just before he commenced his retreat northwards towards the mountains and the French frontier, he, Cugat, wanted to save the remnants of the beaten Catalan Army and their womenfolk and children, who would trek northwards with him through the driving snow. 'We know we have been beaten by that base swine Franco. All the same, we must show the world that we Catalans did *not* surrender to the Fascists. We fought to the end, and we were free men until we laid down our arms to the French, and our Catalan brothers in that country.'

The General had faltered, and for a moment could not continue. Cusi was not an emotional man – his English blood ensured that. But at that moment, his Latin temperament took over, and his eyes flooded with tears. Hastily, he pulled

* English Cusi.

5

himself together. In this hour of crisis, there was no time for sentimentality. 'What is it you want me to do, General?' he asked. Outside, it was beginning to snow, and through the cracked window of the peasant cottage which was Cugat's Headquarters, he could see the long line of peasants, some of them barefoot, their heads bent against the driving flakes, laden as they were with their pathetic bits and pieces.

'We have received information from our sources on the coast at Alicante that the German battleship *Deutschland* is about to sail from the port, heading northwards. *Teniente*, can you guess what its objective is?' The beaten, one-armed general hadn't waited for Cusi to answer. He did so himself. The Fritz will bombard our Catalans retreating along the coastal roads – and unfortunately our men, women and children too, if we don't stop the ship—'

'And you want us to stop her, sir?'

Numbly, General Cugat nodded.

Like most regular army of his kind, General Cugat had been brought up to dislike the English. He had been taught they were a treacherous, money-grabbing nation which had destroyed Spain's empire back in the sixteenth and seventeenth centuries. But he knew, too, that an Englishman's word was his bond. Cusi was only half-English, he knew that, as well. But at that moment of crisis, with his life and career ruined, the one-armed general knew he could trust Cusi implicitly. He laid his hand momentarily on Cusi's broad shoulder. 'Thank you, *Teniente*. I know you will do it.'

Without a second's hesitation, Cusi replied, 'I shall, *mi General*.' He had saluted and walked out into the falling snow. He didn't look back. There was no need. General Cugat and his ragged, beaten army already belonged to the past.

Brr. The burst of tracer caught Cusi and his little band of volunteers completely by surprise. Behind them, the slugs howled off the steel derrick in a series of angry blue sparks. 'Hit the deck!' Cusi yelled urgently. 'They've spotted us!'

His followers needed no urging. The Reds had placed a machine crew on the top of the crane opposite. Now its spot-

6

light was creeping towards them, as the gunners prepared to finish the intruders off from their vantage point high above the docks. Cusi knew it. His mind raced as he tried to find a way out and that ice-white circle of light approached ever closer to where they were hugging the damp cobbles of the dock. He need not have worried. Indiano* rose to his feet. He carried the volunteers' sub-machine gun which he had brought back with him from South America.

'Arse with ears!' he yelled angrily. Outlined now in that circle of bright white light, dark eyes narrowed against the glare, he pressed the trigger. The air was suddenly full of the stink of burned cordite. Slugs sped upwards in the same instant that the Soviets opened up again with their Maxim.

Indiano ignored the bullets erupting on the cobbles all around. He kept his finger pressed down hard on the trigger of the sub-machine gun. Up above, the Soviet gunners lost their nerve. They abandoned the Maxim and dived for the cover of the crane-driver's cab. Cusi didn't give them a chance to recover. 'Run for it, boys . . . run like hell!' he yelled above the racket made by Indiano's 'meat-chopper', as he called it.

They needed no urging. They were up and running in a flash. Indiano cursed as his magazine ran out. It didn't matter. The Russians hadn't realized that their intended victims were escaping yet.

With Cusi in the lead, they skidded around a pile of packing cases labbeled '*Moscu*'. A soldier loomed out of the glowing darkness. '*Stoi?*' he challenged in Russian. Cusi didn't understand the challenge. He didn't need to. He paused and lashed out with his right foot. It caught the Russian a cruel blow in the crotch. He went back, rifle tumbling from his hands as they flew to his injured groin. Even before he fell, Cusi kicked him again. He reeled back, gagging on his own vomit, his steel false teeth bulging from his gaping lips.

They ran on. Up in the crane cab, the Russians started firing again. Too late. The Catalans had vanished. By now, soldiers and civilians were firing purposelessly all over the

*Indian. Name given to Catalans who supposedly made their fortune in the Americas before returning home to their native province.

docks. Out in the harbour, officers started to shrill the alarm on their whistles. Hoarse, angry cries rose on all sides in Russian and Spanish. Cusi laughed crazily. The more panic there was, the better. He'd reach his objective quicker that way. With luck, he and his volunteers would be aboard and under cover before the Russians started searching the docks.

Now they could see the naval ships anchored closer to the shore. They were mostly small craft: the water was shallow and not suited for ships with a greater displacement. Not that it mattered much. Most of the Republican fleet – the pre-war Navy had gone over to the Fascists for the most part – had not sailed for months now, as Cusi knew. The Fascists and their German and Italian allies were too powerful; the few surviving ships that had remained loyal to the Government had not dared to tackle the might of the modern German and Italian destroyers and cruisers.

Panting hard, Cusi dropped to one knee. Around him, his Catalans formed a defensive circle. They knew if they didn't find what they sought soon, the enemy would discover them. Cusi peered down the line of warships, mostly abandoned save for a skeleton crew, their plates red with rust, minus even their navigation lights. Then he had it. 'Boys,' he hissed urgently, 'There she is. My old *Vittorio*. She's still in the land of the living, thank God.'

Behind him Indiano muttered cynically, 'Just. What a mess! Do you expect us to go to sea in that old tub?'

Cusi was too delighted to be put off by the criticism. Hastily he said, as a flare exploded just above them and bathed them in its glowing, unreal, icy-white light, 'Not only go to sea, you South American bastard. But to sink the Fritz cruiser *Deutschland* as well. Now come on before our Soviet friends and allies start filling us full of holes.' They began to run again . . .

Two

'*Bitte um Verzeihung, Herr Admiral.*' The *Deutschland*'s captain, flushing crimson instantly, stepped back from the cabin's door, as if its handle was abruptly red-hot. After all, it wasn't every day that the head of the German Secret Service, and an admiral to boot, was caught like this. For Admiral Canaris, head of the *Abwehr*, was reclining on the cabin's horse-hair sofa, naked save for a pair of skimpy drawers, his booted foot between the legs of his African servant, the other pressed against the black man's tight backside, pushing hard, and obviously enjoying every moment of the procedure.

'Come in, my dear Captain,' Canaris cried, waving his hand and swinging back a lock of his snow-white hair, which gave him his nickname in the German Navy of 'Father Christmas' or 'Santa Klaus'. 'Just trying to get these damned boots off before my bath.'

Hesitantly *Kapitan zur See* Patzig did as he was ordered, trying to avoid looking directly at the strange scene. Again he wondered at 'Santa Klaus's' sexual orientation. After all, what was a simple sailor like himself to make of an admiral, who disdained uniform, liked to cook for his subordinates and seemed to take more pleasure in his two dachshunds than his own daughters – and then this strange Moroccan, who spoke no other language than his native Arabic?

Canaris gasped, the boy shot forward, the black boot still clutched between his skinny thighs, and the *Abwehr* chief breathed, 'That's a relief, Captain. Why I ever wear the damned things I do not know.'

Captain Patzig could have told him; wearing boots was prescribed by Naval Regulations when on board ship, especially one that might soon be seeing action. But he didn't. Instead, Canaris sat up and asked, 'Where's the fire, Captain?'

Patzig assured Canaris there was no fire. At the moment, everything on the big battle cruiser and the sea area all around was untroubled. 'Currently we're off Tarragona, Herr Admiral, which is now in the hands of General Franco's troops. The local wireless station informs us that everything is under control there and we face no danger.'

'I see.' Canaris rubbed his genitals as he absorbed the information. Patzig wished the Admiral wouldn't do that; it was embarrassing. 'But carry on, my dear Captain. You didn't come down here when I'm about to take my bath to tell me that.'

'No, sir. It's Barcelona.'

'Ah, the Red stronghold, eh? What's going on there. Have the damned Bolsheviks finally fled for France?'

'Not exactly, sir. As far as Tarragona can make out from their fifth columnists in the Catalan capital, the place is in a state of chaos. Reds are fighting Reds. The peasants from the surrounding countryside are looting, raping and burning mercilessly.' He shrugged. 'From what I've seen of them – most of 'em without a pot to piss in, if you will forgive the expression, Herr Admiral—'

'I will.'

'They don't have the strength for that sort of thing.'

Canaris rose to the bait. He loved to air his knowledge of Spain and the Spanish temperament. 'You will be surprised, Captain, at the depths of Spanish passion, the pent-up resentments of the peasants, the black hate that can turn those humble folk into cold-blooded sadistic murderers—'

'*Effendi*,' the soft voice of the *Abwehr* chief's Moroccan servant broke into the two officers' discussion.

Patzig gasped, a little shocked again. The servant stood at the door of the bathroom, totally naked save for what looked like a baby's diaper tucked between his legs, revealing all too clearly his sexual organs, a snowy-white towel over his right arm. If the servant had ever possessed body hair, it was now shaved off, so that his gleaming black skin was as smooth as some young boy's.

'Ah,' Canaris exclaimed with delight, 'my bath awaits.' He rose immediately, and with a swift movement, discarded his drawers, as if he could not get into the water soon enough. 'I've been looking forward to this ever since we sailed from Alicante.' His smile vanished. 'Keep a weather eye open, Captain. You never know with the Spaniards, Patzig. They are more full of tricks than a pack of monkeys.' And with that, the middle-aged admiral waddled to where his servant was waiting and allowed himself to be wrapped in the bath-towel before the door of the bathroom closed behind him.

For a moment or two, Patzig stood there, shocked and puzzled. Then he realized that he ought to be on deck now that they were closing with Barcelona and whatever dangers the *Abwehr* chief thought might be lurking there. If he, Patzig, had his way, he'd have Canaris court-martialled and thrown out of the service. The man was obviously a disgusting deviant of some kind. All the same, Canaris had the Führer's ear, and Adolf Hitler seemingly relied upon him as his expert in all matters concerning Spain. And in this year of 1939, it was not wise to offend the Führer in any way, even if one was, as he was, commander of Germany's newest and most powerful battle cruiser.

On the bridge, all was subdued efficient calm, with stern-faced, clean-cut young officers carrying out their duties with professional ease. It did Patzig's heart good to see them. He nodded to the first officer. 'Kempfe, anything unusual to report while I've been down below?'

'No, sir.' The first officer hesitated, and Captain Patzig, still annoyed by the scene he had just witnessed in the Admiral's cabin, snapped, 'Well, out with it, Number One.'

'Well, I don't know whether it's important. But—'

'Let me be the judge of that. Spit it out.'

'Signals have just picked up a garbled message from the Russians in Barcelona. It's all total confusion there. But obviously one of the Red bosses thought it important enough to get this signal off to whatever Soviet shipping is out there off the port.'

'Go on,' Patzig urged, suddenly intrigued.

'Well, the message – uncoded, by the way, sir – urged

11

everyone to be on the lookout for a former Republican torpedo boat which has been stolen—'

'*Stolen!*'

'Yessir. Stolen.' Number One looked as puzzled as the skipper. 'God knows why anyone would steal a broken-down tub of a Spanish torpedo boat probably built at the turn of the century, knowing the state of the pre-war Spanish navy.'

Patzig seemed to consider a long time before he responded. He was not a very intelligent or perceptive man. But his years at sea had taught him to 'feel' when something was wrong, even if he didn't understand why. 'If the Reds put out that kind of message to warn their own ships off Barcelona, we can conclude that the people who have stolen this torpedo boat don't belong in their camp, Number One,' he concluded finally.

'Well, I'd say the same, sir,' the other officer agreed.

'If that is the case, what's this missing torpedo boat up to? Is it just another bunch of the Red rats abandoning the ship? But if that's the way it is, why should the Soviets be alarmed enough to send out a warning in clear, eh?'

Obviously Number One had no answer to that overwhelming question. For he turned to the young lieutenant who was navigation officer, reporting now to the bridge with what looked like the latest weather forecast from the *Deutschland*'s met section in his gloved hand. 'Well, Jansen, what is it?'

'Weather worsening, sir. We can expect snow squalls by 0600 hours, and there's mist forming rapidly to a depth of three to six kilometres from the coast. It will worsen the further we go up the *Golf de Leon*.'

'Thank you, *Oberleutnant*,' Number One said, and turned back to a perplexed Captain Patzig. 'Your orders, sir?'

For a moment the captain didn't respond. Instead he stared out at the thickening mist, dripping off the bridge-window and deadening the steady throb of the great warship's engines, face sombre. He shook his head suddenly like a man trying to wake from a heavy sleep and answered, 'All right, we will carry out our mission on the morrow as planned. Admiral Canaris thinks it is of great importance to do so. In the meantime,' he hesitated, 'in the light of this missing torpedo boat – *heaven, arse and cloudburst!*' he cursed abruptly for some reason. 'In this shitting fog, a torpedo boat could launch a tin fish right up our arse and we wouldn't even know she was there until we felt the impact.'

'Sir,' Number One responded dutifully, though he hadn't the slightest idea why the skipper was suddenly so irate.

'We'll post a double deck watch – and put the quick firers on five minutes alert. I know,' he beat Number One to it, 'they won't like having their beauty sleep disturbed, but they are getting an extra allowance for serving in Spanish waters in wartime. Let them lump it.'

'Sir,' Number One said again.

'All right, I'm going below. Call me at the first sign of anything strange.'

'Sir,' the other officer responded for the third time. Then, as the Captain left the bridge, he allowed himself to relax, whispering under his breath, 'Nervous as a shitting old woman.' Then he, too, turned to stare at the rolling grey wall of mist, his keen face hollowed out to a death's-head in the green glow of the bridge's instruments.

Down below, Admiral Canaris felt relaxed; it was as if his usually taut nerves had been bathed in soothing olive oil. As always, his servant Mohammed had given him the relief that he could not find with his own wife. Now the boy had gone to the galley to prepare one of his rice and greasy mutton dishes, while the German cooks, preparing the crew's usual potato salad and sausage suppers complained about the stink of the rancid fat Mohammed used. But that would be about that. No one aboard the *Deutschland*, ordinary rating or senior officer, dare offend Admiral Canaris's servant.

Canaris concentrated once more on the present mission. Settling himself more comfortably in the chair, he considered the plan, which he had agreed on with the Führer himself. The Führer had insisted that it was about time that the *Kondorlegion*[*] and German naval units which had supported Franco's nationalists throughout the war in Spain against the Reds should be withdrawn. Hitler had maintained that he might well need his battle-experienced airmen and naval

---

[*] 'Condor Legion': supposed German Air Force volunteers who, with their new high-performance planes, had bombed their way across Spain in support of Franco.

13

personnel in the north of Europe, and Canaris told himself that he did not need a crystal ball to know what that meant. Hitler was soon going to start the war that he had long planned against Britain and France. His battle-experienced airmen and sailors might well be used to spearhead that blitzkrieg attack.

Thus it was that Hitler had ordered him to inform Franco that he, the Führer, would risk Germany's newest and most powerful battle cruiser to eradicate the Republicans' last remaining army, Cugat's Catalans, or at least stop it reaching the French border as an armed cohesive unit. Naturally Franco had agreed, even after Canaris had exacted a promise from him that he would help Germany if ever a similar situation arose. But then Franco, fat, placid and unassuming as the Spanish general seemed, would do anything if it meant killing the 'Reds', whom he hated with an almost religious passion. For as Franco often declared in public, the 'Republicans were the servants of the devil!' – and he seemed to believe it, too.

Now Canaris told himself that Cugat must have already moved out of the Catalan capital, Barcelona. There was no place there for them. Barcelona belonged to the Soviets. Cugat, with no motorized transport to speak of, would be undoubtedly using the coastal roads, as narrow and steep as they were, to move his troops northwards. Indeed, Canaris guessed as he sat there plotting in his cabin, they'd be heading for the French railway marshalling yards at Port Bou on the border. The mountains to his left flank would protect him from aerial attack under the prevailing miserable weather conditions over the Pyrenees, and Cugat would not be expecting any attack from the sea.

Canaris's dark, hooded eyes sparkled maliciously. And that was where the one-armed Catalan general was wrong. The attack *would* come from the sea. If the *Deutschland* could interdict the coastal road between, say, Roses and Cadaqués with her great guns, Cugat would be stalled. On one side he'd be faced with a sheer drop to the sea far below, and on the other, there'd be the foothills of the Pyrenees. Admittedly there were tracks running up there, but nothing suitable for an army. Cugat's military organization would

14

break down, and his corps and divisions would be reduced to scattered companies, even platoons. And that would be about the end of the Catalan Army as a cohesive, organized force. It would virtually disappear, and the last threat to Franco's takeover of Spain would vanish once the Russian Bolsheviks had fled Barcelona, taking their gold and other loot with them.

Canaris heard the timid knock on the door and knew immediately who it was. Indeed, the smell permeating into the cabin already told him it was his beloved Mohammed. His servant, as always, wanted to share his native food with him. 'Enter,' he called out, so pleased with himself that everything was working out so well in Spain that he might even attempt to enjoy the servant's favours again this night. He deserved it, and in Berlin, to which he must soon return now, he'd have to be more discreet than here in a foreign country.

Mohammed entered, 'Couscous,' he said simply, proferring the steaming bowl of food to his master.

But Admiral Canaris was not fated to enjoy his servant's couscous this night, nor for that matter, Mohammed himself. For in that very same instant, the telephone on the wall started to buzz urgently, and even before he picked it up, the head of Germany's Secret Service knew that it signalled trouble – serious trouble . . .

Three

Cusi shivered violently. He didn't know if it was nerves or just the damp fog, which was rolling in ever thicker, wet, cold and somehow sad. Out at sea, the Soviet freighters heading for home were beginning to sound their foghorns at regular intervals. It was like the moans of lost souls. He shook himself and tried to shrug off the strange mood that seemed to afflict him. He guessed it was something to do with the fact that he knew this was the end of Catalonia for the time being. After what he was going to attempt to do, he could never go home, while that fast swine Franco ruled, at least. Now he would face exile, as would the men who were supporting him, Indiano, Jordi and the rest. But despite that knowledge, they were prepared to go ahead with their risky mission. Cusi forced a smile. They were good men: the best that his native country would offer.

Carefully he opened the throttle. In his mind, he was working out his tactics. Once the *Deutschland* had cleared the general area of Barcelona and started to come closer to the coast still held by General Cugat and his retreating army, he would strike. It would have to be a quick in and out. Surprise would be everything. He couldn't risk the German ship coming to full alert. Once her deck guns started to bear down on the antiquated torpedo boat, it wouldn't be long before the Fritzes blew him out of the water. He had no doubt about that. The only ally he had at present, apart from surprise, was the thick fog.

By now he had almost decided where the best place to ambush the *Deutschland* would be. He had picked a spot somewhere between Alt Empordà and Roses, though he thought probably he'd attack at Roses, just in front of the

16

little ruined castle on the coast itself. He'd come out from behind the cover and go hell-for-leather for the German battle cruiser. He had only four torpedoes, on which Jordi, the religious one, was still working furiously. So he'd have only one chance. If he missed the first time, the Fritzes would give him the full benefit of their deck artillery, and he had an uneasy but certain feeling that the old *Vittorio* wouldn't survive long then. He picked up his loudhailer and called, '*Jordi, val?*'

Jordi wiped the rain and sweat from his brow with the back of his oil-smeared hand and cried, '*Val, Angles.*'

On any other occasion, Cusi would have smiled at Jordi's use of his first name. Even now, after knowing his Catalan volunteers for years, in some cases, and speaking their own language with them when he was better used to Castilian Spanish, they still didn't regard him as a true son of Catalonia. He was still the Englishman, or at least part of him was. But now Cusi had no time to dwell on the stubborn nationalism of his own crew. The moment of confrontation was getting ever close. For he had already calculated that he was getting closer to Alt Empordà, and the enemy battlecruiser couldn't be far behind. 'All right, Jordi, arm the tin fish!' he called through the megaphone.

'*Clar*, Angles . . . I'm doing so already.'

Cusi nodded his satisfaction. He could imagine the tension that was now sweeping through his motley crew of former coastal fishermen and ex-members of the defeated Republican Navy. They knew as well as he did that they were only going to have 'one bite of the cherry', as his poor dead mother might have said. If they failed the first time . . . Cusi stopped short. He didn't want to think that particular thought to its logical and unpleasant end. Instead he concentrated on the wheel, and what lay before the old *Vittorio* . . .

'*Scheisse . . . verdammte Scheisse*,' Canaris cursed angrily as he stood next to Captain Patzig on the bridge of the *Deutschland*, peering into the foggy dawn as the wipers ticked back and forth over the glass with squeaky inexorability. 'But how does our man in Barcelona know? I mean, I know the Spaniards are fatalists – they are fascinated by death. But even a dyed-in-the-wool Spanish fatalist surely wouldn't risk his neck attacking Germany's most modern warship in an antiquated torpedo boat armed with four torpedoes! That goes beyond all my concept of the Spaniard gained in years of study of the country.'

Patzig shrugged. Let Canaris think what he liked, but he was responsible for the *Deutschland*, which the Führer himself had named and launched in Hamburg only two years before. It was he who would be punished if anything happened to the pride of the German *Kriegsmarine**. 'All I can say, Herr Admiral, is that our man in Barcelona has risked his life to find out this information for us – and he has discovered something which I haven't mentioned yet.'

'What?' Canaris demanded.

'This, sir. The man, Cusi, who stole the *Vittorio*, won a medal back in 1937 when the war here in Spain broke out by tackling a battleship which had gone over to the Nationalists – single-handed. I know she was old and slow and his boat was faster and all that, Herr Admiral. But this rogue Cusi did hit the *Jaime I* and put her out of the conflict for some months. That's the kind of fellow the Wop bastard is. And I don't want my *Deutschland* to be damaged in the same way because I didn't take the right precautions.'

'*Schon gut*,' Canaris snapped angrily, knowing that his hand was being forced by the 'nervous Nelly' standing next to him. 'I take your point. I see you have already taken some precautions – the double watch, the gun crews standing by, etc. Now I suggest another, Captain Patzig.'

'What is that, sir?'

'We send up the seaplane. It can act as our eyes and ears. It could give us ample warning of any attack for – say – a distance of a couple of sea miles of the *Deutschland*, even in this fog.'

Captain Patzig looked shocked. 'But the fog, sir. Visibility's down to a couple of hundred metres at best. And besides, sir, the seaplane could easily stray off course in such a pea-souper, and if one of our pilots landed among the wop rebels . . .' He shrugged eloquently. 'They'd shoot him out of hand.

* German Navy.

18

They have no concept of the rules of war or the Geneva Convention.'

Canaris was tempted to say, in his most biting manner, 'We are *not* at war with Spain – and since when have we observed the Geneva Convention here in Spain?'* But he desisted. There was no time to waste. 'What does the fate of one pilot matter against that of a thousand men on board this ship? Captain, send up the seaplane-spotter right away.'

'Sir.' Reluctantly, Patzig touched his hand to his gold-braided cap and went off to carry out the order, leaving Canaris to his own thoughts. They weren't particularly pleasant. Five minutes later the double-winged seaplane came racing down from the deck of the *Deutschland*, gained height ponderously before rising into the dawn fog. For a moment or two, those on the bridge could hear the roar of its twin motors, and then there was silence, the plane being swallowed up by the fog, which seemed to be growing ever thicker.

Patzig shook his head like a man sorely tried. Things were going wrong; he could feel it in his bones . . .

Swiftly Cusi cocked his head to one side as the little torpedo boat ploughed steadily through the dawn mist, everyone available now on deck, peering through the rolling clouds of wet fog, eager to catch the first glimpse of their prey. At first he thought he was mistaken. The *mist* often played tricks like that. It distorted sound; it magnified it too. And if one were an imaginative person, it made you believe there was sound when there was none.

But then he heard the steady throb-throb once more, and he knew he had heard correctly the first time. 'Indiano,' he called softly, as if the enemy was only metres away, trying to pick up his words.

'*Teniente?*'

'Stand by with the Hotchkiss. I think we've got visitors.'

Irreverent as ever, Indiano bowed stiffly at the waist and

* The German Condor Legion was notorious for its bombing of Spanish cities and the indiscriminate murder of Spanish civilians.

said in formal Spanish, as if he were some high-born regular officer, '*A su servicio, mi Commandante.*'

Cusi said something rude and then concentrated on the sound. It was that of an aircraft engine. The plane, whatever it was, was flying at stalling speed just above the fog, and Cusi knew why. It was looking for something, and, as Jordi crossed himself, as he always did at such moments of high tension and impending danger, Cusi knew who it was searching for. His little *Vittorio*. But to what enemy did the plane, still unseen, belong to? To the Soviets, or to the Fritzes on the *Deutschland*?

As the seconds passed leadenly, with every man on deck tense and apprehensive, the wet fog trickling down their hard, unshaven faces like tears, Cusi considered what he should do if he spotted the plane, or it him – something he prayed at that moment wouldn't happen. Whether the plane belonged to the Soviets or the Fritzes, it would be equipped with radio, as most planes were these days. Once the unknown pilot had identified the *Vittorio*, he'd contact his base on land or on sea immediately. In essence, they had only a matter of minutes, perhaps even seconds, to knock the bastard out of the sky and make a run for it before the pilot could give a correct reading on their position.

Cusi licked his lips, which were suddenly very dry. He knew it was due to nervous tension. But nervous tension kept a man on his toes in battle, and now he needed to be ready for action instantly. Nerves tingling electrically, he listened to that ominous throb-throb above him as the unseen plane circled and circled, waiting to spot its prey like some metallic hawk . . .

Leutnant zur See Jansen was very young – he had only recently graduated from the *Marineakedemie* – and anxious to do a good job. After all, a full admiral and Captain Patzig personally were waiting expectantly for his report. He couldn't let *them* down. Behind him in the observer's seat, *Obermaat* Ziemanski, however, did not seem to have a care in the world. Instead of getting on with his job of observing, he was waffling away about the red-light district of

Hamburg's Reeperbahn and how the price of the whores there had gone up since the Führer had taken over power six years before. 'In them days, Lieutenant, you could get a decent pavement-pounder for a couple of Reichsmarks. Now, it'd cost a poor old seaman a month's hire to do a mattress polka with the girls – and, mark this, Lieutenant, you have to provide yer own Parisian.' He meant contraceptive. 'It's something to do with the shortage of rubber. They say Fat Hermann* needs all the rubber he can get for his new Four Year Plan.' Ziemanski sniffed. 'Mind you, I bet he don't go short of rubber. Him and the poison Dwarf† have got all them film stars to chose from. They'll need rubber aplenty—'

'Please, *Obermaat*,' a frustrated Jansen broke in finally. 'Can't we concentrate on the job?'

'Only trying to keep you entertained, Herr Leut—' The petty officer broke off abruptly, his craggy drinker's face suddenly animated. Very businesslike now, he cried, 'To port, sir . . . There's a gap in the fog . . . I think there's a boat down there, sir!'

Instinctively Jansen pushed the joystick forward, hardly knowing that he was doing so. He went into a steep dive, heading straight for the gap and the patch of grey-green, sullen water below. Behind him, Ziemanski spun his machine gun round and clicked off the 'safety'.

In that same instant, Cusi on the little bridge spotted the plane, crying, 'On to him, Indiano . . . It's a German!'

It was. Cusi identified it from the recognition tables he had learned as a young naval cadet before the war, in what now seemed another age. It was a Dornier 17 seaplane of the type used in Germany's largest ships for reconnaissance purposes. The plane came from the *Deutschland*. That was for certain.

Indiano didn't need to be told that. Indeed, when there was a chance to fire and kill, the former South American immigrant didn't require orders. He didn't wait for Cusi. He tucked the heavy butt of the French machine gun into his right shoulder

---

* The grossly fat Hermann Goerring, Minister and Head of the Luftwaffe.
† The undersized Doctor Goebbels, known thus on account of his height and his vitriolic tongue.

and, barely seeming to aim, sent a stream of tracer zipping upwards. In a kind of lethal Morse, the heavy bullets ripped through the mist towards the slow-moving plane.

Leutnant zur See Jansen reacted. Too late. Instead of diving into the stream of bullets as an experienced pilot would, he panicked. '*Great Crap on the Christmas Tree!*' Ziemanski cursed. To no avail. In his overwhelming fear, Jansen jerked the nose of the little plane upwards. It slowed the Dornier to almost stalling speed. Worse the manoeuvre exposed the whole of the seaplane's blue-painted belly to the enemy. Only for seconds, but it was long enough.

Below, Indiano kept on firing, his dark eyes filled with the blood lust of battle. The slugs ripped the length of the Dornier's unarmoured belly. Great chunks of metal flew to left and right. The fabric severed everywhere. Wires broke and dangled abruptly in a series of violent blue sparks. The plane's nose tilted.

At the controls, blood pouring down the side of his ashen face, Jansen fought to keep the Dornier airborne. His breath came in great, panicked sobs. Behind him Ziemanski yelled, dropping the butt of his own machine gun, 'Keep her nose, you silly bastard . . . In three devils' names!'

To no avail. Jansen, at the end of his tether, was losing the uneven battle. A savage burst ripped his chest apart, stitching blood-red button holes from one side to the other. He screamed, and flung up his arms in a gesture of absolute agony and despair.

'*THE CONTROLS!*' Ziemanski shrieked.

But it was too late. Next moment Jansen slumped over his shattered controls, dead or unconscious. It no longer mattered. Trailing a stream of cherry-red flame behind it, the little seaplane commenced its dive of death, with *Obermaat* Ziemanski frantically grabbing for a parachute that no longer existed . . .

Four

Things happened fast now. They had to. As the Dornier bobbed on the surface again for a moment and Indiano, grinning broadly, took careful aim and killed a floundering *Obermaat* Ziemanski, still screaming for mercy, with a single shot, Cusi on the bridge reasoned there was no more time to waste. He dropped his plan to ambush the *Deutschland* as she sailed close to the coast off Roses. He couldn't take the risk that she might pull far to sea beyond his range and use her big guns on Cugat's retreating Catalans. He guessed from his own experiences in the Republican Navy that it would be German standard operating procedure to monitor the radio signals from the dead pilot of the Dornier every few minutes. Now that he had gone off the air, the German commander would probably have realized that the spotter plane had been downed by enemy action. If the Fritz had come to the first conclusion, he might well have decided that it would be safer, with such a large target under command, to withdraw further into the Mediterranean, or break off the action altogether until he received total air cover from the *Kondorlegion* at their base south of Valencia. Whatever he decided, Cusi guessed the Germans would be expecting his attack; and he, for his part, knew that attack could only succeed if he had the cover the fog offered the *Vittorio*.

Thus he pulled out all the stops now. Risking collision with any damn-fool fisherman who might have decided to venture out from the many small fishing ports that dotted that part of the Costa Brava, he opened up the throttle. The *Vittorio* shot forward. Despite her age, she reached twenty-five knots within minutes. Her every timber seemed to vibrate under the strain. The instruments shook and trembled. She seemed to strike every wave as if it were a solid brick wall, and he could feel the old familiar blow in his guts that he remembered from a light craft going all-out, which was invariably followed by a sensation of nausea. But on this occasion, he didn't mind the sudden desire to vomit, as an evil-tasting bile flooded his throat. For now he was animated by a burning feeling of revenge for the terrible years that lay behind him and Catalonia: against the 'Frog'* and his nationalists and the foreigners, the Moors, the Germans and Italians which the arrogantly styled *Generalissimo* had brought to Spain to win his revolt for him.

More by instinct than real knowledge, he steered his little craft on a south-easterly course; his loyal Catalonians grouped themselves to either side of the bridge as the torpedo boat seemed to skim over the sea. They held on the best they could, their clothes soaked with spray, buffeted every few seconds by the icy waves which flew high to right and left of the prow. Cusi didn't seem to notice. His attention, just as theirs was, was concentrated on the first sighting of the enemy ship, his mind racing frantically as he planned his attack. For he was under no illusions. Once the trained gunners spotted him, they'd open up with a tremendous barrage. Experts that they were, all of them regular naval personnel, they knew they couldn't allow the little torpedo boat to get into the 'dead ground' where they couldn't bring their guns to bear. That would be fatal. The Catalans could slip them a tin fish at close quarters, and all they would be able to do would be to take their revenge when the enemy emerged from the dead ground once more and tried to escape. Then it would be too late.

Suddenly, startlingly, the fog lifted. It was if some god on high wanted to give this puny David a final chance on this winter's morning. And there she was. The Goliath, rearing up in front of the speeding craft like a solid cliff of dull steel. The sight took Cusi's breath away. He had not realized up to now how large and impressive the most modern battle-cruiser in the whole of the German fleet was. But there was no time to ponder that now. Already Aldis lamps were

* A nickname, based on Franco's appearance, for the dictator.

beginning to blink a bright white on the upper deck of the *Deutschland*.

Even as Indiano yelled, 'There's the big bastard!' and Jordi crossed himself yet again, Cusi could faintly hear the ship's klaxons shrieking their warning and see tiny figures running along the *Deutschland*'s decks, striking their gongs to alert the off-duty watch. All along the port side of the great ship, gun turrets started to swing round menacingly as the German gunners prepared to take up the challenge. The moment of truth had arrived.

Cusi reacted with the same daring skill that had helped him to torpedo the *Jaime I* at the beginning of the war. As, on the deck, the torpedoes were prepared for their final running, he threw the little craft from side to side. She twisted and turned crazily. Great waves swamped her deck. Twice, it seemed, the radio mast would hit the heaving water to both sides. It didn't, for Cusi was exerting all his skill and cunning.

A siren howled. A star shell burst overhead. It was followed by another, and yet another. The torpedo boat was drenched in a brilliant, glowing, unreal white light. The crew rushing about their duties looked like ashen-faced ghosts. Cusi didn't notice. His whole attention, his whole being was concentrated on the German warship. It was as if he had lived his whole life hitherto for this moment.

Tracer started to zip towards him. The German gunners were ranging. In a minute, the bullets, which lashed the water all around the *Vittorio*, would be followed by shells. Still Cusi held to his course. A pom-pom battery of heavy machine guns opened up with a steady *thump-thump*. The heavy machine gun shells exploded all around the flying craft. The mast was hit. It went over the sides in a mess of crackling angry blue flames. In front of Cusi, the glass protective screen crumpled into a glittering spider's web. Almost automatically, hardly seeming to notice, Cusi smashed the glass through with his elbow, the blood spurting up from the lacerations almost immediately. Again, Cusi didn't notice. '*Tally ho!*' he yelled exuberantly, as he remembered his poor dead tortured mother doing at moments of high excitement, and opened the throttle to its widest extent. The *Vittorio* surged forward even more, shaking violently, as if she might fall apart at any moment.

The first heavy shell exploded some fifty metres to the front of the speeding craft. For an instant, she disappeared beneath the geyser of the wild whirling water. Any observer might have thought the *Vittorio* couldn't survive that terrible maelstrom. But she did: she emerged from it and kept heading for her target.

On the deck, the torpedo hands, undeterred by the shells which were beginning to fall all about, the red-hot razor-sharp shrapnel hissing frighteningly through the air, slicing the *Vittorio's* timber into matchwork, were almost ready now. But Cusi still did not order them to fire. His gaze was fixed hypnotically on that steel cliff ahead of him, her port side ablaze with flame, as the German gunners fired all-out knowing it was vital to stop the puny little bastard before their attacker achieved the dead ground.

'*Heil Hitler*,' Indiano yelled crazily, as he flung up his arm in the very same moment that Cusi yelled over his shoulder at the torpedo mates, '*Fire one . . . Fire two!*'

The speeding craft shuddered. There was the hiss of escaping compressed air. A splash. The first container of a ton of high explosive slid into the wild white water. The second followed. Cusi didn't wait to see if the torpedoes were running straight and true. He'd leave that to the torpedo mates. He broke to left in a great swirl of water, which rose like two mighty swan wings to his left and right. Just in time. A salvo of 57mm shells burst just where he had been. Then he was racing away at full speed, mentally counting off the seconds he estimated it would take the two tin fish to reach the battlecruiser if they were running on a true course.

'*Three . . . four . . . fi—*'

His count was violently interrupted by a great explosion. His face was slapped by the blast as if someone had struck him with a flabby, damp fist. He flung a wild glance over his right shoulder, already half-knowing he had been successful. He had. A great jet of scarlet flame seared the length of the *Deutschland's* port side like a giant blowtorch.

Already her grey paint was beginning to bubble and pop. Here and there living torches, screaming hysterically, were starting to throw themselves over the side into the sea below in their unreasoning panic. Slowly, the German warship started to lose speed.

On the deck of the wildly trembling *Vittorio*, his men were cheering, crying the name of their lost homeland over and over again in triumph. It seemed that all their sense of loss, their frustration at the last months of terrible slaughter, their knowledge that even if they escaped the Germans' revenge now, they would never see Catalonia again, found expression in that primeval cry of victory.

The young skipper had no time for such matters at that moment. One glance told him that although he had not sunk the *Deutschland*, he had crippled her temporarily. General Cugat's Catalan army would be safe this day, or for many to come.

Now, however, he had to ensure that his brave volunteers would be safe too when they made their break for the coast. How? He made a split-second decision. The German gunners, their blood up now and angry at what this puny David had done to the *Deutschland*, would be waiting for him as he emerged from the dead ground and made his dash to escape. They'd attempt to blast him out of the water, and with such massed firepower at their disposal and ready and alert at their battle stations, they would undoubtedly succeed. How could he fool them, catch them off guard for the vital minutes that he would need to speed out of range and disappear into the still-lingering dawn fog? Then he had it. 'Torpedo mates – ready the two fish for a stern shot.'

'Stern shot?' Jordi queried over the noise coming from the stricken German warship – the wail of the klaxons, the angry bellows, orders and counter-orders, the chatter of the machine guns like the work of irate woodpeckers, with all the while the searchlights sweeping the water to the ship's port side, trying to find the ship which had inflicted such grievous damage on the pride of the German *Kriegsmarine*.

'Get on with it!' Cusi snapped. There was no time for explanations now.

Indiano guffawed at Jordi's discomfirture. For the religious man was sensitive despite his months in the front line on the River Ebro. 'Now don't cry, *chico*. Remember, senior officers don't explain their plans to humble little sailors like us.'

Despite the tenseness of the situation, Cusi grinned momentarily and then, assuring himself that everything on the little craft was as ready for the break-out as it would ever be, he cried, '*Tally ho!*' and he was off.

The sudden burst of motors going all-out alerted the Germans high above them that their attacker was moving again. Although he couldn't understand the cries floating down from the top of that steel cliff, Cusi could guess that someone was sounding the alert. '*Los . . . dalli . . . dalli . . . Die Schweinehunde kommen . . .*' Now the crew would be concentrating totally on exacting their revenge. Cusi said a hurried prayer that his ploy would pay off. He knew he would not get a second chance. He pulled the throttle wide open. The craft's prow lifted high out of the water. Twin curtains of wild white water flew up on both sides of the *Vittorio*, and then she was sweeping round the bow of the *Deutschland*, leaving her port side behind and heading for the opposite beam, going all-out . . .

On the quarter-deck, as the fire crews battled the flames, rushing back and forth under the command of hoarse, angry, red-faced petty officers, Captain Patzig was beside himself with rage. '*Heaven, arse and cloudburst!*' he cursed yet again, his face puce, as if he might well have a stroke at any moment. 'How am I going to explain this to the Führer, Admiral?'

Canaris, who had long learned to control his own temper – such outbursts were signs of weakness – said calmly, 'Leave that to me, my dear Captain. Concentrate on sinking the Catalan swine. Then I'll clear it with the Führer. A few medals, a public ceremony honouring our brave boys in Berlin—'

'In three devils, Admiral, why should I be interested in shitting medals in shitting Berlin—' He never finished his angry ranting. For the guns on the port side had not opened fire despite the fact that he, too, had clearly heard the engines of their hidden attacker burst into frenzied activity. He pulled the plug out of the bridge speaking tube. 'Guns,' he rasped after whistling down the brass opening, 'what's the matter with your gunners? . . . Why aren't they opening fire?'

'Because, sir, the enemy—'

But the rest of the gunnery controller's words were lost in the great cry that rose from half a hundred young sailors' throats on the *Deutschland*'s starboard side: 'there she is, the shitehawk . . . There's the bastard. She's going to do a bunk . . .'

Five

Almost immediately, two of the *Deutschland*'s upper deck searchlights flashed on. Desperately the marines manning them tried to cone on the little craft far below, seeming to skim effortlessly across the surface of the sea on the stricken ship's starboard side. '*Um Himmelswilen,*' their lieutenant cried, 'get the swine!'

Cusi knew nothing of this. All he knew, with a wild glance behind him, was that the Germans were trying to pinpoint him for their starboard beam gunners, who so far, caught by total surprise as they had been, had not yet opened fire. Soon they would, and then he would have to pull his last trick, and if that didn't work, then, as Indiano would have said, 'be calm and make a handsome corpse'. But it hadn't come to that yet, and by God, if he had his way, it wouldn't. With all his energy, nerves ticking excitedly, the adrenalin pumping furiously, he opened the throttle as wide as it would go.

The searchlights coned him. It felt as if he were feral lynx in the border mountains, caught in the centre of a hunter's telescopic sights. In a second, the gunners above would focus on that killing cone and start pumping shell after shell at him. Desperately, he tried to shake off the light. Sweat glistened on his forehead. Unconsciously he hunched his shoulders, as if he half-expected the first red-hot piece of shrapnel to strike there at any moment. His breath came in short, sharp, hectic gasps.

Behind him at the rear of the *Vittorio*, Jordi crouched over the last two 'fish', gaze fixed hypnotically on the bridge. His hand hovered impatiently over the firing mechanism. He knew only too well that split-second timing counted now.

There was a sharp crack. The first quick-firer had zeroed in on the fleeing craft. A tracer shell zipped flatly through the air. Next instant it exploded in a geyser of whirling angry water to the craft's rear. '*One*,' Cusi cried to no one but himself. He knew the drill. One shell to the rear. One to the front. The third would hit the *Vittorio*, and a direct hit would blow the old torpedo boat right out of the water. Sweating even more, face grim, a blue vein bulging crazily at the side of his temple, he zig-zagged more wildly.

Above on the upper deck, Patzig slapped his thigh. '*Grossartig*,' he yelled. 'We've got the swine . . . Come on, you shitty gunners . . . Finish him off, will you!'

Next to him, Canaris remained silent. He could not be infected by the enthusiasm and emotions of other people. Even now, when he, too, wanted revenge on the Spaniard trying to escape below, he had to keep the feeling to himself. That had to be the way he functioned. So, apparently calm and controlled, he awaited the outcome of this duel between David and Goliath wordlessly.

Patzig continued to shout and curse, while below, those who had no duties to carry out, yelled and whistled and clapped their hands like a pre-war football crowd cheering on the teams of Bremen and Hamburg. But at the holed and shattered controls of the *Vittorio*, Cusi didn't see this as some peacetime contest. Half English though he might be, he had enough hot Latin blood in him to know that this was a game with a lethal outcome. Someone was going to die in the next few minutes, and if he, Angles Cusi, had his way, it would not be his loyal Catalan volunteers. Half turning, he bellowed above the snap and crack of the quick-firers, as the closest gunner prepared to fire his next ranging shot, 'Jordi . . . fire three and four!'

Jordi didn't hesitate. This time he didn't even waste a second crossing himself as was his custom. He pressed the firing levers. Concentrating on zig-zagging as close as he dared to the bow of the great ship, Cusi felt the boat shudder and lighten a little as number three and then number four torpedoes hit the water. Then he was out in the open sea, feeling as if he were completely naked and totally vulnerable, for now he was clearly exposed to the angry gunners of the *Deutschland*.

The Germans were not slow in making the most of this beautiful target; it was as if the enemy had just been presented to them on a silver platter. A wall of fire erupted from both sides of the great ship's bows. Tracer spat from the heavy machine guns. It sped towards the fleeing craft like glowing golf balls, growing larger by the instant. Scarlet flame erupted from the heavier guns. Someone was even firing mines at them: great barrel-like cannisters of high explosive which rose into the air a few metres and then came crashing down, to explode in huge sprays of angry water.

Cusi seemed to bear a charmed life as he swung the craft from left to right, disappearing under the water only to emerge a few seconds later unscathed, the deck behind him flooded with water, the crew drenched. But he knew his luck wouldn't hold. Tragedy would strike at any moment. Now, as he held the wheel with his frozen hands as if his very life depended upon it, he started to count off the seconds of the torpedo run. At that distance it could take only three seconds at the most for number three fish to strike the *Deutschland* and bring that murderous fire to an end. Three passed. *Nothing!* The torpedo had missed. Behind him, Jordi, stop-watch in his hand, cursed violently and then commenced praying with all the fervour of the novice monk he had once been before the war.

Cusi yelped with sudden pain. Shrapnel hit and bored into his left shoulder as if someone had just thrust a red-hot poker into his flesh. He faltered. For a moment, he thought he might black out with the agony of it. Just in time, he caught himself and clung desperately to the wheel, trying the best he could to continue his violent zig-zagging.

Suddenly, startlingly, there was a great roar behind him. He turned his head with what seemed to him incredible slowness. Yellow smoke was pouring from the stern of the battle-cruiser, and her speed was decreasing even more. Number four had hit her. Cusi's heart leapt with joy, even though a strange black cloud seemed to be about to envelop him. He couldn't understand it. He blinked his eyes rapidly. His vision cleared again.

A vivid scarlet flame rushed upwards. There was a clearly audible creaking and rending of tortured metal. It was as if the battlecruiser's steel had developed a voice. The towering superstructure of the *Deutschland* started to waver and tremble like a live thing. Hastily Cusi blinked his eyes once more to clear his clouding vision. Up on the lookout tower, a panicked sailor had dived from the mast. He came sailing down like some professional high-diver at a pre-war swimming pool showing off his prowess. Suddenly he realized he had missed his distance. He started to flail his arms, as if trying to ward off the inevitable. He failed. Next moment he slammed into the steel deck below and crumpled in a heap of broken bones like a burst sack of wet cement.

In that same moment, Cusi blacked out. He, too, crumpled to the deck, and then Indiano was fighting furiously to free Cusi's vice-like grip on the wheel, and the *Vittorio* was surging forward once more with the South American at the wheel, roaring all-out for the nearest patch of fog and safety. Behind them, the bow of the *Deutschland* dipped deeper into the debris-littered water and slowly, but inevitably, she came to a stop. On the quarter deck, supporting Captain Patzig, who seemed to have suffered a heart attack, waiting for the surgeon lieutenant to hurry from the wounded below to attend to the *Deutschland*'s captain, Canaris swore an oath in his mild, totally controlled manner: 'I shall avenge this. They will suffer.' He had recognized the class of torpedo boat which had just inflicted the crippling blow on the *Kriegmarine*'s pride and joy. It was the old '*Moewe*' class, which the old-time Imperial Navy had been forced to get rid of after Imperial Germany's defeat by the victorous and vindictive Allies at the end of World War One. Spain had obviously obtained it. It would not be too difficult to find out who in the Spanish Navy had been trained in that class. One thing would lead to another, and his agents in Spain would ensure that those concerned would not live to see the end of the year of our Lord 1939. He was certain of that.

'Red bastards,' he cursed under his breath. 'You'll rot in hell, mark my words.' Then he dismissed the matter and concentrated on the dispatch to Hitler and the *Caudillo**, as Franco was calling himself very grandly these days, as soon as the signals office below was cleared of its wounded . . .

Indiano, who had taken over command of the *Vittorio* while Cusi lay bleeding and unconscious, made a quick decision once they were safely under the cover of the fog which still lingered along the rugged coastline of the Costa Brava. 'Comrades,' he announced. 'We're losing fuel and I don't like the look of Angles either. So we land and attend to both.'

There was a murmur of agreement from the weary veterans, soaked, hungry and not a little shell-shocked from what had just happened. 'Then what, Indiano?' Jordi asked. 'Where then?'

Indiano shrugged eloquently. Despite the stress of the last hours, he had not altogether lost his sense of humour. 'God knows, Holy Man. Why don't you go down on your knees and pray for divine guidance?'

But his supposed sense of humour didn't work. The crew looked as downcast as before, so he said, '*Bon*. We head for the nearest harbour, and if God *is* on our side, as you seem to think, Holy Man, he will reward us with at least a good whack of *pa amb tomaquet*†.' He licked his thick lips in anticipation. 'That is, if the peasants haven't scoffed even the tomatoes!'

They hadn't.

As the local doctor attended to Cusi's wound, finishing off his ministrations with two injections, the bent-backed old women, the only women left in the coastal village (for it was expected that when Franco's troops entered, they'd rape any woman up to the age of sixty) fed the ravenous volunteers with the simple dish. The bread was stale and the olive oil was sparse and rancid, but they ate it with an appetite, washing it down with greedy slugs from the skin-covered flasks of

*Political and military leader, generally at the head of a personality cult.
†*Pa amb tomaquet*. Bread with tomatoes. A cheap Catalan peasant dish of bread smeared with tomato paste and garnished, if available, with olive oil.

local wine, as if they knew this was the last time they would ever taste the wine of their homeland.

The doctor, a fat, dirty man who peered through cracked pince-nez glasses and whose beard, as grubby as he was, was cut in the style of the nineteenth century, patted Cusi, who was already beginning to stir, saying, 'You can't stay long here. The enemy is not far off. One of their planes on reconnaissance came over just after first light.'

Indiano nodded his understanding, and with a belch of appreciation said, 'But you're staying, doctor.'

The old doctor nodded at the black-clad crones in their shawls. 'The women. Who knows?' He didn't make his meaning any clearer. But they understood, and Jordi, who was now feeding Cusi a mixture of wine and water said, 'But they'll kill you, perhaps, sir. You could come with us. We could use a doctor.'

The old man smiled wanly. 'I've lived long enough,' he answered with typical Catalan fatalism.

'But we haven't,' Indiano snorted, rising to his feet, adrenalin helped by the food and wine flowing through his veins once more. 'There are adventures to be had, women to be enjoyed, money to be made, doctor. We're not ready to die yet, are we, comrades?'

There was a murmur of agreement from the others.

The old doctor looked at them as if he were seeing them for the first time. He nodded his head. 'Of course, you're right . . . Young men never think they're going to die. I—'

He never finished. Up the street, where the last cottages vanished into the snow-covered foothills, there came an urgent cry of warning. '*Cavalry*, lads . . . *enemy cavalry* . . .'

Next to the bearded doctor, the old crone who had brought them the food flung her apron in front of her wrinkled face and cried, 'The Moors . . . the Moors are coming . . . They'll rape even old women . . . God in heaven . . . *Los Moros!*'

The young men knew what she meant. It was a fear that dated back to the Middle Ages. Whether the legends were true or not, these simple peasants along the whole coastline of Spain feared the Arabs who had invaded their country back in the eighth century. The tales, handed down from generation to generation, were horrific, full of cruel torture, pillage and sadistic sexual rapine.

Now they could hear the clatter of horses' hooves, muffled a little by the slush and snow, and told themselves that it could only be Moorish cavalry. Franco had brought the 'Moors' back to Spain, after their having been driven out of the Iberian peninsula centuries before, when he had invaded Spain from Morocco in '36. But if the old woman was terrified out of her wits by the knowledge that they had returned and were approaching her remote coastal village, the Catalan volunteers weren't. They weren't prepared to make a stand and defend the place. But they were ready to give the unsuspecting Arabs a bloody nose while they readied their boat for their journey up the coast to neutral France.

Like the veterans they were, they prepared a rough-and-ready ambush while Cusi, supported by Jordi, helped to fill up the *Vittorio*'s fuel tank with diesel from a small Renault tank, presumably abandoned by General Cugat's Catalan Army as it had struggled north. Hastily they scattered soup plates in the verges, covering them with earth and slush so the Arab scouts might take them for mines and be forced into the centre of the cobbled village street, where they would be an easy target for their sole Hotchkiss machine gun. Others of the volunteers entered the cottages lining both sides of the street, clambering into the haylofts of their upper floor, where they knocked the tiles to the ground, poking their weapons down at the approach road, while under Indiano's direction, those of the village women who weren't too shocked to do so prepared twisted bundles of straw soaked in petrol they had taken from an abandoned broken motor-cycle to make a primitive kind of Molotov cocktail, of the type introduced into Spain by the Soviets. It would suffice, they reasoned, to frighten the cavalry's horses and make them shy and rear up, unsettling their riders in the same moment that the ambush sprang.

Then all was done, and as the old women shuffled off the best they could for the cover of their own cottages and the old doctor took shelter next to Cusi and Jordi by the *Vittorio*, his battered old leather instrument case at the ready to treat

36

any casualties, a strange brooding silence fell over the little *pueblo*, broken only by the cautious clop-clop of horses' hooves as the Moors approached. The scene was set, the actors were in place, the drama could commence.

Six

The sound of horse-hooves had slowed down now. Cusi, crouched next to the *Vittorio* with the other two, knew why. The Moors were seasoned troops. Some said they were the best Franco had under command. Certainly he always used them as his shock troops. As brave as they were, they were not going to ride straight into a trap. He guessed their Spanish officers, trained in the mountain fighting against the Riffs in Morocco*, and now against the Republican irregulars in their own country, would be cautious, even though the coastal village looked abandoned by Cugat's troops.

Up in the furthest cottage, Indiano let go of the former owner's pride and joy, a tethered goat. It was the signal, as it snorted and clattered down the cobbled street towards the little jetty. The Arabs were just round the corner. If their scouts saw the goat, it wouldn't alarm them. It might even convince them that the village was empty, and that the goat had broken loose and was searching for water. Besides, the goat promised meat, and the Arabs loved their mutton and goat meat. He waited. Next to him, the doctor ran the scalpel the length of his dirty palm, as if to test its sharpness for the amputations soon to come. At any other time Cusi might have made an ironic comment. Not now, however. He was in no mood for irony. The situation was too tense.

Up ahead, the first Arab had appeared. He was mounted on a fine white horse, his rifle slung over his cloak, as if he might not need it after all. But he was obviously on the alert. Leaning low in his burnished ornamental saddle, he stared at the mounds made by the slush-covered soup plates in the

* The long, protracted fighting against the mountain Arabs, where Franco had made his reputation and become Spain's youngest general.

verges, dark, hawk-like face suspicious. Then he rose in his silver stirrups and shouted to someone behind him in accented Spanish: '*Mines.*' He had concluded that the plates really were mines. He tugged at the horse's bridle and edged it swiftly into the centre of the cobbled street. Now he made a perfect target.

A moment later, another couple of horsemen appeared. This time, one of them was an officer – and Spanish. Instead of the Moors' turban, he wore a forage cap with a golden tassle hanging down the centre of his fine, aristocratic face. Over his shoulder, he carried a silver sabre. To a waiting Indiano, he looked the typical Fascist aristocratic grandee who had brought so much suffering to Spain and Catalonia since Franco had started his civil war. Carefully, very carefully, seemingly hardly daring to breathe, he brought his Hotchkiss to bear on the officer. Centimetre by centimetre, he brought the machine gun into position, until the steel sight neatly bisected the unsuspecting officer's arrogant face. 'Now, my fine gentlemen,' he muttered to himself, 'enjoy your last breath of our good air . . .'

The Spanish officer waved his sword. It flashed momentarily. Behind, the body of the riders appeared. All of them were armed with carbines which they kept slung across their backs, as though they expected no trouble despite what they thought were mines in the verges. The officer turned to his front. He tugged at his bit. The stallion reared up on its hind legs, as if it was some trained beast about to commence the celebrated Spanish ritual.

Indiano laughed to himself. Gently, he took first pressure, squeezing the Hotchkiss's trigger, his dark face set in a bitter grin.

The cavalry started to trot on again. Next to Cusi, the bearded doctor muttered 'Poor young men,' and opened his medical bag wider as if in anticipation of the bloody business to come.

The tension rose. Jordi started to mutter the 'Hail Mary'. But all the same, he kept a tight grip on his pistol. They came ever closer. Cusi hissed in Spanish, '*Madre de Dios*, why don't they open fire?'

That very next instant his wish was granted.

With a savage grin on his face, Indiano pressed the Hotchkiss's trigger. At that range, he couldn't miss. The officer tugged at the reins of his splendid mount. The horse came to an abrupt halt. It was almost as if the stallion was as puzzled as its master. For the officer's haughty, arrogant look vanished, to be replaced by one of bewilderment, as if he couldn't understand why this was happening to him. Slowly, very slowly, the gold-tasselled forage cap slipped down his face. He seemed powerless to stop it, though it made him look absurd. Then suddenly, surprisingly, he let out a shrill, hysterical scream. A gigantic fist appeared to propel him from his mount as Indiano's savage burst of machine-gun fire ripped his chest apart, and then he was rolling on the cobbles in the mud and slush, writhing from side to side in agony, while all around the horses of his squadron trampled up and down upon him. The slaughter had commenced.

Five or ten minutes later it was all over, though to Cusi, watching the massacre like someone viewing a newsreel safely in a cinema, it seemed like an eternity. Now the old crones, equipped with cracked, chipped enamel buckets and basins, were hobbling out of their cottages, carving knives ready to hack pieces from the dying horses – the first real meat that some of them might have seen for months, perhaps even years. While they set about their grisly work, sawing and carving, the volunteers went among the fallen riders, kicking those who were feigning death, slashing open the pockets of the real corpses, looting them of their cigarettes and chocolate, swiftly blowing the backs of their skulls off afterwards to make sure they were really dead.

A sergeant was brought up. He was a Spaniard too, but as dark and swarthy as any Moor. Probably he was from Andulusia and had Arab blood in him. But he was not as stoic as his subordinates. He was trembling and fearful. He constantly attempted to go down on his knees and clench his hands together in the classic gesture of supplication. Under Indiano's leadership, he didn't get a chance. He was cuffed mercilessly, cursed and sworn at; and one of the cronies

40

paused in her carving at the flank of a still-living horse and, waving her bloody knife, threatened as if she might well cut off his genitals there and then.

A little weakly, Cusi gestured to Indiano to bring their sole prisoner over to him. He felt no charity for the terrified Spanish sergeant. He hated the 'Moors' just as much as his men did. But he needed some information, so he lied, saying, 'Tell me the truth and your life will be spared, *Sargento*.'

The prisoner's relief was palpable. He gave a great sigh of relief and attempted to kiss Cusi's blood-stained right hand, crying, '*Gracias . . . gracias a Dios, Don*—' His cry ended in one of pain as Indiano kicked him hard in the ribs, snorting, 'Hold your water, you bastard.'

Cusi wasted no more time. He asked one sole question, and then he knew they'd have to flee. The Arab cavalry would be the forerunners of the lorried infantry to come. 'How far are your nearest troops from here? Speak. Quick!'

The sergeant was obviously pathetically grateful that his life was apparently being spared. His Adam's apple running up and down his skinny throat, he said, 'Anything, sir . . . Anything.'

'Get on with it. *Pronto*.'

'More than two kilometres, sir,' the prisoner quavered. 'The snow and the road is holding them up. The Cavalry can move better under those conditions—'

'Planes?' Cusi interrupted him curtly.

'Forgive me, sir, I know nothing of the planes, sir. They are the Germans' . . .'

But Cusi was no longer listening. Indiano realized they had got all they would out of the prisoner. He knew, too, that Cusi had promised the sergeant his life. But he thought differently. Let the sergeant survive and he'd be running off at the mouth to the rest of the Fascist swine as soon as they arrived at the village. He pulled out the dead officer's pistol, which he had just looted, and without appearing to take aim, pressed the trigger. The sergeant screamed and fell into the snow, blood gushing in a bright red arc from his skinny chest, dead before he hit the ground.

Minutes later the *Vittorio* was on its way again, belching

41

smoke from the tank's diesel oil. Slowly the battered old craft headed for the open sea, beginning the final stage of its voyage into exile. Behind, the bearded dirty doctor stared at the village street: the dead officer lying on his back in the snow, his mount nuzzling its master's dark face, as if it couldn't comprehend why he didn't respond; the shot sergeant still leaking blood into the slush; the old crones busy cutting slices from the horses and slopping them into their pails and buckets – the whole misery of war-torn Spain encapsulated into this one village street. '*Pobre Espana*,' he moaned to the dull, overcast sky in anguish . . . '*Mi pobre Espana*!'

They passed Port Bou some two hours later. From where they lay out to sea, the throbbing of the overheated engine subdued for a few minutes as they took their last look at their homeland before they headed on to Nîmes and French exile, they could just see the smoke rising from the many locomotives waiting to take more refugees and survivors from the beaten Republican Army to the French internment camps.

They stared transfixed in silence. Even the snow flurries blown out to sea by the icy wind coming from the Pyrenees didn't disturb their earnest contemplation of their last sight of Catalonia. What thoughts went through their heads, no one could guess. But even hard-bitten Indiano had tears in his eyes, and they were not caused by the icy cold.

Cusi was as the rest. He had thought before that he would be able to say a few words to his volunteers at this moment: something that might comfort them, give them some hope for the future. But now he found he was unable to do so. His mind was too full of the past: a boyhood spent in those same mountains with his mother, telling him tales of a far-off England; his father, the worthy, much older *abogado* in his huge nineteenth-century office in Barcelona, so solemn that he felt he ought to call him 'sir' instead of 'Father'; his days as a naval cadet sailing the length of the Costa Brava in his own little craft with not a care in the world, happy to be alone with the deep blue sea and burning sun of the Catalan summer; even the war, when he had gone into battle against Franco's Fascists, confident that this time they'd break the power of the Madrid generals and be allowed to rule their own province in peace, speaking their own native tongue, bringing prosperity to all, middle-class citizen and humble peasant alike.

Now that dream was shattered, and the young half-Englishman could not find the words to express his feelings and give the men who were following him into exile some sort of hope that one day they might return to their beaten homeland. For there was no hope. The Fascists had succeeded in Italy, then in Germany, now in Spain. He gave up. Without saying anything to his crew, he returned to the bullet-shattered bridge and opened the throttle. Slowly the *Vittorio*, which had fought and won its last victory, started to chug northeast on its way to Nîmes. Behind, Port Bou and their homeland disappeared into the snow storm. Before them lay the unknown.

BOOK TWO

Exile

One

There was the clatter of horses' hooves which the pudgy little French admiral had been waiting for. He nodded to his adjutant. Hurriedly he crossed the big eighteenth-century room with its gilt furniture and sketches of men-of-war, dominated by the admiral's hero, Admiral Villeneuve. The admiral was important, very important, indeed, he was a minister of the French cabinet. But he was as of nothing, the handsome young adjutant knew, in comparison with the old man whose arrival was now heralded by the squadron of the *Garde Républicain* now clattering into the courtyard of the Ministry of the Navy below.

Admiral Darlan pulled on his heavily gold-braided cap and glanced at his image in the great mirror. He patted the cap and was satisfied. Besides, the great old man now arriving did not hold much with such frippery, he knew. 'Show,' he was wont to snort, with remarkable force for such an old person. 'Bah, all show!'

Outside, the *Garde* had halted. The kettle-drummers on both sides of the great steps which led up to the ministry started to beat the '*rappel*'. They rattled away furiously until the order came for them to stop. Now the waiting admiral could hear the cheers of the spectators, gathered outside the railings. '*Vive le marechal*!' they cried . . . '*Vive Marechal Petain.*'

As the band of the *Garde* struck up the 'Marseillaise', Admiral Darlan could hear the officer of the navy guard call to the sentries to stand to attention. There was the crisp stamp of nailed boots on the steps. The Minister of War, Marshal Petain, the Hero of Verdun*, the saviour of France, some said, was on his way to the Admiral's great office. Suddenly Darlan, as vain and brimming with self-confidence as he was, felt uneasy. 'How do I look, Jacques?' he hissed at the adjutant. 'Am I all right?'

'Perfect, sir,' the other responded as the two of them heard the slow steps of the Marshal and his adjutants coming along the corridor outside. After all, the Marshal was in his eighties and naturally slow.

The great Rococo doors were flung open. A flunkey bellowed at the top of his voice, 'The Marshal of France, Marshal Petain!'

Although they were of similar rank, Darlan was so impressed by his illustrious guest that he clicked to attention like a raw recruit and saluted.

Petain, simply dressed in his marshal's uniform, one sole medal adorning his chest, touched his hand to his own *kepi* momentarily, and said in the thin, reedy voice of a very old man, 'Thank you, Darlan.'

Hastily the adjutant pushed a gilt chair to the rear of the Hero of Verdun. The latter sat down on it without looking behind himself. It was obvious that, ever since he had been plucked from a Parisian brothel back in 1916, an obscure, semi-retired general, to rescue the French Army, he had been used to having his every wish catered to. He breathed a sigh of relief, and said quietly, 'Pray, Darlan, please have your office cleared. I want to speak to you alone.'

Hastily Darlan rapped out an order, and as the great doors were closed and they were alone, he said, 'Marshal?'

Petain took his time, in the fashion of very old men, though his gaze still had the same fierceness which had frightened the mutinous soldiers of Verdun so long before. Finally he said, 'I am displeased, Darlan.'

Darlan looked anxious. Had he incurred the Hero's displeasure because he had objected in the Senate to the Army receiving more money to augment the Maginot Line, which Petain supported?

---

* In 1916 when it seemed the French Army might mutiny after two years of war, the Marshal had rallied the troops by using draconian methods including mass executions, and finally beaten the invading Germans at Verdun.

He need not have worried. The Great Man had come to see him on another matter entirely. Petain said, 'I wish you to keep this confidential, Darlan, at least until the President announces it personally, but I am now to be the new ambassador to Spain. Now that Franco has declared himself chief-of-state, it is felt that we French have to accord him someone of importance as an ambassador. Someone who can balance that rabble of the Popular Front*. As I am a military man, and as Franco and I both represent views opposite to those of that Red rabble of Blum and his like in the National Assembly, I have been chosen for the position.'

Darlan breathed an inner sigh of relief. He had not fallen out of favour after all. 'Congratulations, Marshal,' he enthused. 'What a great honour!'

Petain took a long breath, and Darlan could hear the old man's breath wheeze deep down in his lungs. Despite his age, Petain was not prepared to retire to the country and enjoy his last few years on this earth. The Hero of Verdun still felt it his duty to save France from the new enemy. This time it wasnt the *Boche*; it was the Reds and those decadent scribblers, journalists and the like, who supported the Popular Front.

'It is clear, Darlan,' he continued, 'that those fools the English and their tool here, Premier Daladier, will go to war with Herr Hitler and Germany soon. Mussolini of Italy will soon join in on the German side, and our poor France will be facing not only the Germans and Italians, but also possibly the Spanish too. A two-front war, in other words.' He let his words sink in before adding significantly, 'That would be a disaster for France. The Republic wouldn't survive. We might well end up just another Soviet.'

Darlan nodded his agreement. He, too, feared the Communists and the fools who backed them in Paris. 'But if I may say so, Marshal, what has this got to do with the Navy?'

'This.' The answer came with surprising speed. 'I hear from my sources in the *Deuxieme Bureau* –' he meant French Intelligence – 'that those Spaniards – all Reds, naturally –

---

* National Front, the 1930s grouping of the French left-wing parties.

who attempted to torpedo the German battleship *Deutschland* have sought and have been given asylum down in Southern France, where they are under the protection of your Navy.'

Hastily Darlan said, 'On the orders of the Government itself. I would have no truck with such Red types personally, Marshal.'

'Of course, of course,' Petain said soothingly. He knew what a vain man the little Admiral was. 'However, with your help it would make my position easier in Madrid – and appease Herr Hitler, too – if we could assure General Franco that we have taken care of the Spaniards.'

'How, sir?' Darlan hesitated before saying softly, as if he feared saying the words aloud. 'We – er couldn't eradicate them, as I personally would wish. It would be all over the left-wing press here in Paris twenty-four hours later.'

'Of course not,' Petain agreed. 'I understand your dilemma. However, I would like to suggest that these Reds have their craft destroyed, and that they, and all former Spanish naval personnel in France, should be removed from the frontier camps and transported secretly to isolated areas in the far north, well away from Paris. Say, in the Alsace-Lorraine region. I mean, who goes to that God-forsaken area save the *Boche* during their periodic invasions of our poor country?' He paused and licked his dry lips meaningfully. Hastily Darlan nodded to his adjutant. Within seconds, a silver tray bearing glasses and a bottle of fine old cognac appeared, as if by magic. Darlan personally poured a glass for the old man, and then one for himself. He raised his glass and said, '*À la votre, M'sieu le Marechal.*'

For the first time, the Hero of Verdun smiled. It was the cautious, wintry smile of a very old man who knew he should be long dead, but who had hung on somehow, and now viewed life warily, as if he expected that it would play some life-or-death trick on him if he wasn't very careful. 'Thank you, Darlan. You are kind.' He bent with an audible creak and breathed in the cognac's bouquet appreciatively. 'Now I have given up women and food, it is one of my last pleasures, Darlan.' Next moment he tossed back the fine old brandy like he might have done as a young officer swallowing a glass of cheap rotgut. He gasped. 'Then it is done, Darlan. You will get rid of those Red scoundrels. As far as the Spanish and their German and Italian allies are concerned, those murdering scum have been quietly eliminated. *D'accord?'*

'*D'accord,*' Darlan agreed, drinking his cognac more slowly, as if he were mulling over the problem of Cusi and the crew of the *Vittorio* very carefully indeed.

Thus they sat, the two most important military figures in France, indirectly plotting against their own country and its British ally. Soon they would wield great power, together with the powers which would defeat their '*belle France*'. But it would come to nothing. Before the decade was halfway over, one would be dead at the hand of the assassin, and the other in exile, his reputation in tatters* . . .

The poor battered *Vittorio* had limped into Nîmes on the first of March 1939. On their way there, Cusi had dodged a French naval patrol boat for fear that the French Navy, which was supposed to be traditionalist and right-wing, might turn him back right into the hands of the Spanish Fascists. For that reason, he had slipped in and out of the small bays and inlets of that part of the French coast until they now had reached the eighteenth-century port, which was too large for the French authorities to get rid of them without causing a stir.

It was a fine morning as the *Vittorio* limped in, watched by a curious crowd of locals drinking their *rouge* or coffee at the waterside cafés, and further back, in the harbourmaster's office, by a hard-faced official through his binoculars.

Cusi was unable to assess the mood of the watching civilians – were they in sympathy with these Spanish refugees, or did they fear that the newcomers would compete with them for the local jobs which were hard enough to get as it was? But after all that Cusi and his Catalan volunteers had been through in the last few years, he was determined not

*Darlan would be murdered by a French patriot in North Africa, and Petain, the head of the pro-German Vichy Government of Unoccupied France, would be sentenced to life imprisonment in a French island fortress.

to be intimidated by the silent crowd. He and the rest would show the French what true Catalans were made of.

As they tied up and the *Vittorio*'s hard-pressed engine gave one final heartfelt throb as if it were glad to be allowed to die at last, Cusi called as cheerfully and confidently as he could under the circumstances, 'Jordi, the pipes!'

The 'holy man' knew exactly what the skipper meant; the crew, too. As shaky as their legs were after being so long at sea, they sprang lightly to the jetty while Jordi blew the first notes of the Catalan *Sardanes*. Without a signal from anyone, the men formed up in the large circle and silently began the folk dance.

To the onlookers, who didn't know it, the traditional dance must have seemed like the movement of an animated clock that ran in both directions. Slow steps to the left; slow steps to the right. Left . . . right . . . left . . . right, with arms held tightly to the side. Faster steps. Now the hands were slightly raised. Even the ungainly seamen seemed almost graceful as they swayed to the tempo of the pipe, increasing in speed all the time.

The onlookers relaxed. Their faces became animated, although the pipe music must have seemed strange and prim-itive to most of them. Here and there a few of them attempted to hand-clap in time to the music. A few children among the crowd even tried to join in, but the dancing men appeared to be in some kind of a trance and didn't notice. Perhaps they were concentrating too hard on the intricate steps of their native dance, oblivious now to the French.

But not for long.

Suddenly, startlingly, a harsh whistle shrilled once, twice, three times. A hoarse official voice commanded. '*Arretez . . . ça suffit!*'

Jordi's shoulders sagged. He let his pipe drop. The music stopped. In a kind of rough phalanx, a dozen men in the uniform of the *gendarmerie* were pushing their way through the crowd, their tough faces red and angry beneath their steel helmets. At their head was a big, swaggering brute of a *sous-officier*, his fist clutching the polished black-leather pistol holster at his waist, as if he wouldn't hesitate to use it if necessary. '*Arretez!*' he bellowed once again.

The absent look vanished from the faces of the dancers. It was replaced by one of concern, even fear. The Catalans might not understand the French, but they understood the threatening gestures well enough. They were in for trouble.

They were. This was going to be the first contact with official France for most of the abruptly crestfallen Catalan refugees. It was not to be the last. As Angles Cusi told himself with a sinking feeling, using the English expression he had learned from his poor dead mother, for there was not an equivalent in his native Catalan, they had fallen from the frying pan into the fire . . .

Two

Their French jailers, for that was what they really were, called it the '*drôle de guerre*', and he'd soon learn from the Scots who would be taking over from the French in that sector of the Front that they named it 'the phoney war'. And it was a true description of the new war in the west. For after the hectic first days of September 1939, when the Anglo-French armies had mobilized after Germany had invaded their eastern ally, Poland, nothing happened. The Catalans had expected, just as the French all around them in the Saar area had expected, fierce fighting to break out in that remote, rugged country at once. Local civilians had fled in panic, clamouring for weapons to fight against the German Fascists who might invade across the nearby border at any moment. Cusi himself had written a petition in his best schoolboy French, asking for him and the rest to be armed and given French uniforms at once. 'We are all trained soldiers, experienced in war,' he had written for the rest to sign, 'and would deem it an honour to die, if necessary, for the *gloire de la France.*' But France, that first week of September, was seemingly not going to allow them the privilege of dying to achieve some of that 'glory' now ready and waiting for the '*grande nation*', as Cusi had phrased it.

Their petition went unanswered. Instead, the French huddled in their Maginot Line fortifications down in the bowels of the earth. Those who worked above ground and were not allowed the honour of wearing the 'shrimp' badge on their berets to indicate that they belonged to the Maginot élite, went about their jobs with sour faces, half drunk most of the time on the ration *pinot*, unshaven and insubordinate. Not that their officers cared much. They had been wrenched from their comfortable civilian jobs as clerks, schoolteachers and the like, and they were not one bit interested in making real soldiers of their unwilling conscripts. Their only concern was their weekly visit to Metz and the other great cities of the area, to feed their faces, enjoy the luxury of a hotel bathroom and, if they were so inclined, to enjoy the favour of the whores who had now flooded the front line area.

Now as 1940 approached and nothing had happened here in the 'front line', save that the English had moved in to be trained by the French and had caused the first fatality of the war on that front – a frustrated sentry had shot a civilian emerging from the deep woods of the area after he had not answered the sentry's repeated challenges (the Frenchman, it turned out, had been deaf), the Catalans settled down to their back-breaking routine once more. It consisted of chopping down the local pines and shaping them into staves to support the trenches that the newly arrived English were building between the squat concrete Maginot Line fortifications, watched by the bored French 'shrimps'.

Not that the English up there for 'training' in the French art of modern warfare were really English. As Cusi explained more than once when his Catalans said they didn't know the English wore 'skirts' – they thought they all wore dark striped suits, 'melons'*, and carried umbrellas against the persistent rain of their island country, 'All English are not English. Up in the north of that country, there are English called "Scots". They wear skirts because they cannot afford trousers. They make them themselves, and you must never call them skirts. These Scottish Englishmen call them "kilts".'

His Catalans had liked the sound of the word. At odd times when they had their breaks in the frozen forests, Cusi would find them practising 'kilt', rolling it off their tongues time and time again, asking him if they had gotten the pronunciation correct, until Cusi had become heartily sick of the word. Still, it did provide a link between his Catalans and the Scots whenever the two groups encountered each other in the forests in that hard winter, the coldest in a quarter of a century. Both would emerge at the end of a winter's day,

* Bowler hats.

mud-stained and weary, the Scots with their rifles slung, their wet kilts dragging around their hairy knees; the Catalans equally mud-stained and weary, with the latter crying, '*Bonjour, M'sieu Kilt*' – to which the Scottish infantry would yell back, 'Shut yer gobs, you foreign bastards!' in a normally good humoured way, throwing the Catalans the tins of rationed pilchards they disliked and the fish-starved Catalans loved, and the 'tab-ends' that all the Scots seemed to carry perched at the corner of their ears.

And both groups were united too in their dislike of the French, surly, unshaven and not a little drunk, who lounged everywhere in the abandoned villages to the rear, seemingly with all the time in the world on their hands; for, unlike the Scots and the Catalans, they never appeared to work, but hung around waiting for their food and the generous issue of crude, potent red wine which kept them drunk till the next issue.

The weary Scots, the ribbons of their Glengarries blowing in the wind, their naked legs red-raw from the freezing cold, would yell, 'Frogs, make luv with yer lips!', whereupon they'd make sucking noises until some NCO or officer would command harshly, 'Now, none of that, men . . . March to attention!' and they would shoulder their picks and shovels and pass through the muddy village as if they were on parade, leaving the Catalans to grin at the French *poilus'* discomfiture.

But as the winter finally started to relax its grip on that remote border country, with the German villages a mere couple of kilometres away on the other side of the wooded hills, Cusi, the veteran, started to feel a new urgency about this forgotten 'fighting front'. Now fire-fights started to occur almost nightly in the depths of the forest. As March 1940 gave way to April, German patrols ventured into the villages themselves, and Cusi noted that the Germans were taking prisoners instead of shooting the odd *poilu* and afterwards looting his body for identification and indication of his unit.

Once, indeed, the Catalans were awakened by German machine-gun fire close to the wire of their own camp, and the French Senegalese who guarded them, panicked and had to be kept at their posts by their officers with drawn pistols.

That night by the light of a flickering candle, after the panic had settled down and the Senegalese giants were back sleeping in their watchtowers, Cusi faced his men as they slumped or sat on their bunks behind the blacked-out windows of their wooden hut and said, 'Comrades, we must make plans.' He glanced around at the circle of their worn, half-starved faces in the flickering yellow light of the candle, waved back and forth by the draught. 'Perhaps if the Fritzes do come, it might be a blessing in disguise for us.'

'How . . . plans?' Indiano snapped in his new, monosyllabic fashion, for this last year in exile in Northern France had seemed to erode his old vivacity and spirit.

'I shall tell you, if you'll listen,' Cusi answered patiently.

'We're listening, Angles,' Jordi said, as gentle as ever.

'I don't need to tell you that when the Germans come, the French will not put up much of a fight. Even those 'shrimps' of theirs will probably bury themselves in their bunkers and sit it out until the time to surrender comes.'

Several of his listeners nodded gravely, but didn't speak. After months of nothing, it seemed as if something might be happening at last; anything that would help them out of this place and offer new hope.

'These Scottish-Englishmen will fight, I know. My mother used to say the Fritzes feared them in the Great War. The Germans called them "the ladies from hell".'

'Yes, like Annemarie,' Indiano mumbled. He meant the local whore who serviced them occasionally when they had collected enough money among themselves to pay her and bribe the greasy so-called cook who smuggled her into their camp of a Saturday.

'But what have they to fight with?' Cusi continued, ignoring the reference to the whore, who he used himself, though he was ashamed of doing so when just about every one of his Catalans had used her at one time or another. 'Just rifles and bayonets and a few machine guns, and the Germans are supposed to have hundreds of the most modern tanks on their side of the border – and we all know about the Fritzes' modern weapons,' he added bitterly.

A few of them nodded gravely, thinking of the *Deutschland*, which was sailing the high seas again as if nothing had happened to her.

'Besides,' Jordi said, raising his voice above the cold whisper of the wind, straight from Siberia, which rustled and crackled through the frozen pines outside the little internment camp, 'those kilts have their division further back. Once the trouble starts, I'm sure they will return to their division, and then there will be no one here to stop the Germans.'

'Exactly,' Cusi snapped, trying to check the note of rising excitement in his voice, 'and we, comrades, must be ready for that day when the front here collapses and it is every man for himself.'

'How?' someone asked.

'As unarmed civilians, comrade, we don't stand a chance. We'll just be a nuisance to both sides. The French might shoot us out of hand, and undoubtedly the Germans would do so too once they learned what we did back there off Roses.' He paused, let his words sink in for a moment, before saying hastily, 'We must be in uniform. We must look like bona fide soldiers withdrawing as a disciplined formation under orders.'

'Kilts?' Indiano snapped. 'I cannot wear the skirt. How could I? I am a man.' He sat up stiffly.

Cusi gave a stiffled laugh. 'I think not. The kilt wouldn't suit you with your legs, Indiano. No, as French soldiers. I wager that half of the local French soldiers will be tugging off their uniforms and hurrying home to mother, once the Germans fire the first shot . . . So this is what we do . . .'

That first shot, when it came, though they were expecting it, came as a complete surprise. For it was not that of an infantryman's rifle firing a bullet; it was a 37mm high explosive shell discharged from the turret of a camouflaged light tank which came blundering out of the May forest, snapping the pines to its front like matchwood, to grind to a muddy halt only kilometres away from where they were spooning down their morning ration of soup, sipping the thin, watered red wine which was their daily ration.

Indiano cursed. Cusi silenced him with a swift, 'Duck . . . into the undergrowth!' for he realized that the tank commander, now pushing back the turret hatch, had not yet spotted the workers resting in the middle of the forest.

Like the veterans they were, they reacted at once. They ducked into the undergrowth, crawling on their bellies deeper into the forest, while Cusi covered their retreat, peering through the vegetation at the young officer who would have made a perfect target, if he possessed a weapon, as he studied his map, the little tank's engine ticking away like a metal heart. Now, in the silence, Cusi could hear the sound of many heavy-booted feet moving their way cautiously through the trees to the rear. It was the follow-up infantry, and he realized now that the *drôle de guerre* was over. This was the real thing. At last the Germans were attacking. *Their* chance had come. It was time that he and his Catalan volunteers began to put their plan into action, before the Germans – or their French captors – dealt with them; and even as he lay there, hardly realizing that he was witnessing the start of the German *blitzkrieg*, a new form of armoured war which would bring half of Europe under German control within the next year, he knew what form that dealing would take: a bullet at the base of the skull, and a kick to tumble their corpses into the nearest ditch.

Slowly, he began to wriggle back to where the others lay, waiting for his orders. 'Comrades,' he hissed, 'let's make a break for it. Half the Fritz army is coming this way. MOVE!'

They needed no urging. Still clutching their axes, which they had already considered they might need soon, they fled backwards, gaze fixed on the way the Germans would come. But luck was on their side. Fifteen minutes later, they were out of the forest and on the track which led to the village.

The place was the way they had predicted it would be if and when the Germans came. On all sides, the French were abandoning their positions. Those who had prepared for this moment – and a surprising number of the *poilus* had – were tearing off their uniforms frantically, their weapons already abandoned. Those who didn't possess civilian clothes were ripping away their badges of rank, leaving their tunics undone and dropping their helmets as a sign they wouldn't fight, but were prepared to surrender. And it was not only the rank-and-file who were preparing to flee the village; their officers were too, save for their colonel. One-armed and wearing the *Legion d'Honneur*, he lay slumped in his office, a black-red bullet hole through his temple.

But Cusi and his men had no eyes for the sole brave man in that panicked company. They were too busy arming themselves and pulling on bits and pieces of French uniform and helmets which would identify them in the rear as fighting French soldiers. They were not going to be shot by the *gendarmerie* as deserters from the front when they cleared the village. They were to appear to be loyal soldiers, separated from the main body by the surprise German attack, marching to the rear to take up the fight against the *Boche* anew, once they came to a stabilized line.

Then they were ready. Cusi paused for a moment and patted the ill-fitting French captain's uniform that he was now wearing, and flung a glance at his 'company'. '*Bon, mes gars,*' he announced in passable French. He turned and cried over his shoulder, as they followed him, rifles at the trail, as if ready for action at any moment, '*Marche ou crève!*'*

'*Marche ou crève,*' they answered in unison enthusiastically.

They were on the move again. In this midst of chaos, confusion and catastrophe, they sensed new hope. It might be a long journey – a very long one – but they felt they were going home again – back to Catalonia . . .

* March or croak

60

Three

It seemed that the whole of eastern France was on the move. Although most of the civilians had yet to see a German soldier in person, the memories of the first *Boche* invasion of 1914 still lingered, and panic reigned every- where. 'The Germans are coming' seemed to be on every mouth. On all sides, the roads were choked with refugees plodding doggedly west in the heat of that hot May of 1940, knowing not where they were going, animated solely by the compulsion to get away before the *Boche* caught up with them and subjected them to nameless savagery.

Anything on wheels was pressed into service, from ancient farm carts to prams, even cars that had run out of petrol, being drawn now by some skinny-ribbed peasant nag bought by the city people for gold or jewellery, for the canny peas- ants with long memories no longer trusted the paper currency. There were bed-ridden invalids being pushed by their sweating, exhausted relatives in long wickerwork baskets on wheels, little children balancing mattresses on their heads against air attack, urging on tiny carts filled with their pathetic bits and pieces being towed by panting dogs; there were married couples dressed in shorts riding heavily-laden tandems, looking like carefree holiday cyclists out for a jaunt, save that the couples wore pans, metal sieves and the like tied to their heads as a kind of primitive helmet.

The panicked civilians were not the only ones clogging the roads, major and minor, heading ever westwards. The retreating French army was too. By now, the *poilus*, sweating and filthy, had mostly thrown away their weapons, aban- doning their horse-drawn artillery so that the horses could move more swiftly. Looting their way along, they thrust their civilian countrymen, old and young, male and female, brutally out of their path in order to escape themselves from the *Boche*, who supposedly were on their very heels. Every now and again, the shrill cry would rise from the disorganized rabble, '*Les Boches – sauve qui peut!*' and they would panic and break into a run.

Here and there a group of regulars, especially those of the Foreign Legion, would attempt to make a stand – only to be wiped out mercilessly by the advancing panzers supported by their 'flying artillery', the death-diving Stuka bombers falling out of the clear blue sky like metal hawks, sirens screeching, dropping their lethal eggs with amazing precision. Behind them they would leave a smoking charnel house, and the churned fields littered with the *kepis* of the Legionnaires from half-a-dozen foreign countries, who had given their lives for *la belle France*.

Cusi and his Catalans had been through it all before. By now, they had commandeered two French army supply carts pulled by young and willing horses. Hastily they had camouflaged them with branches and green foliage cut from the nearest trees. Then, using only third-class, winding country roads spurned by the civilians and soldiers as being too slow, they had proceeded slowly on their long journey west, each wagon carring an 'air sentry', who could – and would – shout a warning at the first sight of one of the dreaded Stuka dive bombers.

Cusi had made a wise decision. He had reasoned that the 'kilts', as his men called the Scottish soldiers of the 51st Highland Division, would also avoid the main roads, packed with the fleeing civilians. As slow as these backwater 'D' roads were, they provided the right cover for trained soldiers, who would be able to move faster along them.

Cusi had been right. Twice before they started to circumvent the great Lorraine city of Metz, he had proof that he was in reality following in the steps of the withdrawing Highlanders. Once it had been the sight of a bunch of 'English-Scots' sprawled in the careless attitudes of the hastily done to death in a ditch. Another time it had been a group of badly wounded Scots housed in a barn draped with crudely made Red Cross flags, who were singing one of their incomprehensible songs to the tune of a mouth organ, waiting for medical assistance that Cusi knew would never come.

They had done their best for the 'kilts', given what French cigarettes they had left over, plus a whole demijohn of rough French red wine (which had cheered them up no end – 'If we're gonna croak it, laddies, we'll be happy on a couple o' drams afore we go') and found that the Highland Division was heading back to the main British Army, which was in Belgium somewhere.

As they departed, waving as long as they could to the wounded already pouring great portions of the rough *pinot* into their square canteens, raising them in a kind of toast to the Catalans, Cusi was pleased at the information just given him. For he was beginning to work out a rough-and-ready plan which might get them out of this French mess. If he and his Catalans proved their worth to the 'kilts', they might take them with them when they returned to England. He reasoned his mother's fighting race would never surrender tamely to the Fritzes as the French were doing. If they were defeated, they would return to England and fight on, come what may – and when they did, they'd need every man prepared to fight the Fascista, as his men were ready to do. Defeat the German Fascists and the English could well turn their attention to doing the same in Spain. It would be a long, hard road, and he dared not even think of all the time it would take, but one day . . .

'One day, sir?' Jordi, perched next to him on the camouflaged wagon, asked in surprise, and Cusi realized that he had been thinking aloud. 'Oh, nothing, Jordi,' he answered, eyeing the long, straight French road ahead. 'Just indulging in a bit of daydreaming.'

For a long time Cusi would be right; the future, the burning hope that he and the rest be able to return to their homeland, would be a dream. Now this May, and for many months to come, the reality would be destruction and sudden death. Indeed, some twenty-four hours after they had circled Metz and found their way to the minor road leading from the Lorraine capital to Verdun, where once the aged Marshal who had condemned them to Northern France and the work camp had achieved his famous victory over the *Boche*, they were confronted by battle at its most bloody.

At the small town of Etain, a long, straggling place on both sides of the road which led up to the heights of Verdun, vaguely glimpsed in the distance, they came across their 'kilts', fighting desperately to hold the German juggernaut. They heard the battle before they saw it. Immediately Cusi recognized the high-pitched, almost hysterical burr of the German spandau machine gun followed by the much slower rat-tat of the English Bren, sounding like an irate woodpecker hammering away at some stubborn tree. In the distance, too, he could make out the rusty grind of tank tracks, and those tanks *had* to be German, for he knew the Scottish infantry possessed no tanks. Indeed, he doubted if they were armed with anti-tank guns, even.

Cusi looked at his men as they pulled their carts to a halt behind the cover of one of the shabby houses, abandoned and bearing the ugly pockmarks of the initial German bombardment. They looked back at him wordlessly, knowing as he did that the 'kilts' were fighting an all-out battle to their front.

Finally, as the firing lulled a little and the smoke of battle began to drift their way, he asked 'Well?'

They knew without further explanation what he meant.

Surprisingly enough, it was Jordi, the 'man of God', as the others called him, who answered for them all. 'Angles, we help the kilts.'

There was a murmur of agreement from the others.

Cusi wasted no further time. '*Bon*,' he snapped, very businesslike now. 'I don't know how strong the Fritzes are and what kind of dispositions they have. But I *do* know that they won't expect an attack from this direction, the way they've just come. So we take them by surprise, and God willing, we'll damage them enough to turn the scales in the favour of the kilts.' He grinned, feeling the adrenalin surging through his body and that heady, unreasoning sensation of young men about to enter battle. '*À l'attaque!*'

'*A l'attaque!*' they echoed as one. Then, abandoning their horses, they moved forward, darting from house to house,

64

the angry snap and crack of the small arms battle growing louder by the instant.

They passed a blazing textile factory. Dead German soldiers hung out of the shattered windows. On the opposite side of the road, the 'kilt' who had sacrificed his life to kill those Germans lay slumped over his Bren gun, the front of his khaki shirt stitched with blood-red buttonholes. Next to him, his mate lay on his side, curved Bren magazine clutched in his hand, not a mark on him. For all the world he looked as if he might be taking a nap in the warm afternoon sunshine.

Cautiously they passed on in single file, hugging the wall, the sound of battle getting ever louder. Too, that squeaky rumble of heavy tank tracks seemed closer, as they progressed up that battle-littered road, with German and Scottish corpses clutching each other in one final, desperate embrace. Cusi frowned. They might be able to tackle German infantry, especially as they were going to surprise them from the rear, but a tank was a different matter altogether. But he kept his misgivings to himself.

Then they came to a sudden halt. They were just behind the main German line of attack. There were coal-scuttle helmets everywhere, peeping above the smoking rubble or seen through shattered windows. Here and there the Germans were still firing at the unseen Scottish defenders. But it was clear to the battle-experienced Catalans that the Germans were preparing for an all-out, and what they probably thought was to be their final one; hence the tank, waiting somewhere to the left, to provide them with covering fire.

NCOs were crawling from man to man, handing out stick grenades, which the assault infantry tucked into their jack-boots or their belts. Young officers who led the assault wiped the sweat from their brows and tapped the long magazines of their Schmeisser machine pistols to ensure that they fitted. Stretcher bearers, who would go in with the attack, hefted their canvas stretchers more comfortably on their right shoulders and tugged stiffly at the Red Cross placards that adorned their chests and helmets in the pious hope that the defenders would realize they were unarmed medics and wouldn't shoot them when they tended the wounded. All was controlled excitement and readiness, with the young soldiers urinating all the time where they knelt: a sure sign of nervousness about what was to come.

Out of nowhere, or so it seemed to the hidden observers, an older officer appeared. He walked upright through the ruins as if he hadn't a care in the world, merely out for a stroll in the hot May sunshine. He smoked a thin cheroot and appeared to be unarmed. Cusi knew the type. He'd been in this sort of thing often enough before. The man was trying to impress his waiting assault troopers, calm them with his studied nonchalance. The older officer, Cusi knew instinctively, would be the one who would lead the coming assault.

It was the opening that Cusi had been waiting for. He turned to Jordi. 'Cover me,' he hissed.

'What—'

Cusi didn't give the 'holy man' time to ask his question. For already he was wriggling his way forward hurriedly, trying to get within range before the older officer reached his assault infantry. He knew that he was taking one hell of a risk. It needed only one of the young officers preparing for the attack to turn round, and he'd spot this intruder in dirty French uniform immediately. Cusi doubted if he would live very long thereafter. But it was a chance he had to take if they were going to stop the assault.

The older officer had paused. For some reason, his cheroot had gone out. He paused and fumbled for his cigarette lighter; the cheroot had to be relit before he reached the assault troops. It was part of his image. It also was the ideal opportunity for the man who was going to kill him.

While the German clicked and whirled at the wheel of the lighter, sending up blue sparks furiously, Cusi whipped the rifle from his shoulder. Swiftly he wound the rifle sling around his arm to steady the weapon. He peered along the sights. He was right on target. The foresight dissected the standing officer's head neatly, right on target, focused on the broad forehead beneath the heavy helmet. He caught a glimpse of a harshly handsome face, dominated by a big, aquiline nose. He took first pressure gently. He knew time was of the essence, but dared not miss now. He'd have time for one shot only. He tried to control his mounting excitement, forcing himself to breathe carefully. To his front, the officer managed the lighter. Suddenly blue flame spurted up from the reluctant apparatus. It seemed to act as a signal for Cusi. He completed his pressure on the trigger. The big old-fashioned French rifle jerked and spat flame. The metal butt slammed painfully into Cusi's shoulder. Abruptly the air was full of the acrid stink of burned cordite. To his front, the older officer's knees began to buckle like those of a newly born foal. The lighter dropped from his suddenly nerveless fingers. His mouth gaped stupidly. The cheroot slipped to the side of his abruptly slack lips, so that the dying man looked like some absurd drunk. A moment later and all the energy appeared to drain from his skinny body, as if an invisible tap had been jerked open.

He hit the rubble and all hell broke loose. On all sides, the cries went up, a mixture of rage, surprise, fear, 'Der Oberst . . . die haben den Oberst umgelegt . . . Der Oberst ist tod.'

Even as he started to crawl back hurriedly the way he had come, expecting to be fired at at any moment, Cusi knew that the steam had gone out of the German attack on the Lorraine village for the time being. The Scots would withdraw while they still had time. Already he could hear the sound of their lorries revving up, mingled with the rusty squeak of tank tracks, as the unseen German panzer began to withdraw, knowing that it would not be needed in the dangerous front line this afternoon.

Half an hour later, Cusi and his happy, grinning Catalans were reporting to a wounded young officer of the Royal Scots, and were being feted with 'fags', as they were soon learning to call the Scotsmen's cigarettes, and great wads of stale white bread and greasy corned beef, which to the hungry refugees tasted at that moment better than the finest *oinzo*[*] that their doting mothers had ever prepared for them. Soon thereafter they were bundled in with the weary and mostly wounded Royal Scots, and were heading westwards once more in the crowded interior of a big three-ton truck.

* Marinated pork kebab.

Four

On the same day that Cusi and his Catalans saved the remnants of a company of the Royal Scots, a regiment so old that it was known throughout the British Army as 'Pontius Pilate's Bodyguard', Adolf Hitler left his battle headquarters on the Franco-German frontier and flew right across France to meet his fellow dictator Francisco Franco on the Spanish frontier at Hendaye.

It was the first time that the two allied dictators had met, and Hitler was determined to impress the victor of the Spanish Civil War with his power and personality. With him, Hitler had ordered a company of the 'imperial guard', his *Leibstandarte*, to be flown in too. Now as Franco, fat, undersized and greasy, strode the length of the company to the rattle of the kettle-drum, he was forced to crane his neck against his stiff white collar to see the faces of the black-clad, helmeted giants, each man of them well over a metre and a half tall. But as Hitler was to learn that day, the only one he would ever spend in Spain, Franco was not that easily impressed. As Hitler would confess wearily to Admiral Canaris afterwards, 'I'd rather go to a dentist to have a tooth pulled than try to get something out of that damned Spaniard.'

For what Hitler, soon to be the conqueror of France, wanted to get out of Franco was his approval of a joint Spanish-German action which would ensure Spain joined the war on the German side, as Italy under Mussolini had just done.

Talking through his interpreter, a giant of a *Herr Doktor* in the German Diplomatic service, Hitler explained his plan to the attentive, but silent, Spanish dictator, who Hitler would have been shocked to learn was nearly a quarter Jewish himself. 'Once we have conquered France, your Excellency,

I am seriously contemplating entering your country – naturally with your cognizance – through the Basque country at the eastern end of the Pyrenees.'

Franco's moon-like face registered shock. Still, he said nothing. 'Again with your permission,' Hitler continued, 'my troops would head for Gibraltar to link up with an airborne assault by my most élite troops on the Rock of Gibraltar.'

For the first time since the conversation had turned to some form of cooperation between the two Fascist countries, Franco spoke. 'I understand, Herr Hitler. With Gibraltar captured, you can dominate the western Mediterranean, and perhaps knock Britain out of the war.'

Hitler's face lit up. 'Exactly,' he responded eagerly.

Franco raised his shoulders in the Latin way, hands extended, and Hitler couldn't help thinking that the Spanish leader looked like some damned wop waiter apologizing for the fact that the soup was off this day. 'But my country is still exhausted from the recent war, Excellency, and there would be many among my people who would be only too happy to have the damned British removed from the Rock after all this time, but who still wouldn't like them to be replaced by the Germans.'

Hitler had been expecting this objection; Canaris had briefed him well on just how touchy the Spaniards were about Gibraltar. He responded at once. 'But it would not be just us Germans, Señor Franco. Your Spaniards would help us in this great undertaking, and once the operation on the Rock was successfuly completed, Gibraltar would be yours – Spain's.'

Franco was obviously not convinced. He smiled in his toothy fashion and said, 'It would indeed be a great triumph for Spain to regain the Rock after nearly two centuries of British rule. But . . .' Again he shrugged in that eloquent fashion of his before objecting, 'But we haven't the men for such an undertaking, and naturally the British navy would start blockading my poor, underfed country yet again. The people in the cities would revolt. They are on very short rations as it is, Herr Hitler.'

Hitler made an attempt to look sympathetic. Afterwards

he confided to Canaris, 'That Spaniard is like a Jew. He wheedles and rubs his hands as if I am a damned client in his pawnbroker's, trying to extract more money from me.'

'I have been informed too, *mein Führer*,' Franco continued, while Hitler racked his brains angrily for some way to convince the little Spanish dictator to join him in the assault on the Rock, 'by my own people in our Legation in London, that if there was any attempt on Gibraltar, the English would immediately occupy the Canary Islands. That would cause a great deal of trouble in Spain itself.' He flashed his big white teeth, in a look that could mean anything.

Hitler tried again. 'But *Caudillo*, I know it is your stated policy to recover Gibraltar and maintain Spain's colonies in North Africa. It would be our primary aim to help you to do so.'

'That is true, Herr Hitler.' Franco shrugged once again, as if he would like to go along with Hitler's wishes, but was unable to do so due to circumstances beyond his control. He added, 'Perhaps we need more time to work out more positive means of carrying out this operation, *Mein Führer*.' And there the discussions came to an end.

But the two dictators showed no sign that their discussions had been fruitless as they emerged into the brilliant, blinding sun of Spain. The *Leibstandarte* clicked to attention and swung their heads woodenly from left to right as the two dictators passed slowly down the ranks of the black-clad giants. The bands played the Fascist hymns 'Cara al Sol' and 'Deutschland über Alles', and Franco and Hitler embraced as if they were the greatest of friends. It was all over in a display of warm friendship, though the viewers in the crowded, smoke-filled news cinemas were not to know that the meeting had achieved nothing . . .

As the record broke into the National Anthem and the afternoon crowd at King's Cross ABC Cinema rose dutifully from their seats and came to attention, most of that mix of civilians and soldiers were impressed yet again at the apparent power of the dictators, in particular that of 'Old Adolf'; they seemed to be winning the war everywhere.

70

One of that audience, who had entered the newsreel cinema to wait for their trains or enjoy fifty minutes of rest and relaxation in a soft plush seat for sixpence, was definitely not impressed. Indeed, the sight of the two dictators embracing in the hot Spanish sunshine which he knew so well made him angry.

Slowly he followed the crowd outside into the London mid-afternoon gloom. He felt a sense of guilt. He should have been working on his piece for the BBC, scheduled for that same evening. Yet the 'scribbling', as he called his scripts, seemed totally unreal in a world that was falling to bits all around him. It all seemed so purposeless. He wanted to be in the action, doing something to stop the triumphant march of Fascism. Hence his constant visits to the cheap newsreel cinemas when he should be working. There in the smoke-filled fug of the packed fifty-five-minute cinemas, he had a fleeting feeling he was there where the 'real' war was. Of course, he knew it was a delusion. Still, he could not stop it.

He lit another cigarette, and immediately his damaged lungs acted up as the pungent smoke crept down to them. The fit of coughing racked his emaciated body, and he had to stop and lean against the nearest wall to steady himself. A woman passed carrying the usual box gas mark over her shoulder and a baby complete with 'dummy' in its mouth. 'Disgusting,' she muttered. 'At this time of the day. Ought to be in the army serving king and country – a young man like you.' She sniffed indignantly and went on her way.

Under other circumstances, the tall, thin BBC man with the trim, regular army moustache would have laughed. But at this moment, he wasn't in any position to do so. He had once served King and Country, and only two years before he had been shot in the neck in battle fighting the Fascists in Spain. But he had not the breath to tell the woman with the baby that, even if he had been prepared to do so and she to listen.

'All right, mate?' asked the old newspaper vendor with the placard proclaiming the latest wrapped around his legs with a bit of string. 'Need a hand?'

The tall man shook his head and then recovering his breath

said a little weakly, 'Many thanks, old chap. But I'll be all right.'

The newspaper vendor grinned. 'Posh bloke oughtn't to be hitting the wallop at this time of the day. Don't look good to the working classes.'

The man smiled. 'I suppose it doesn't.' He glanced at the scrawl on the poster. *Dutch Army Surrenders . . . Rotterdam Horror, the Reason.*

The vendor saw his look of dismay at the information and said hastily,' 'Don't take it to heart, sir. It's only the *Daily Mail*, and yer knows what them conservative newspapers are like. They're allus crying stinking fish.'

The tall man nodded his understanding and passed on, wishing the Cockney news vendor was right. But he guessed that this time, that Tory paper, which he had hated because he considered it and the *Times* had been the voices of the capitalist appeasers, had got it right. The front in the west was crumbling rapidly under the German onslaught. He told himself that soon Hitler would be the master of northern Europe, and the other Fascists, jackals like Italy's Mussolini, would soon attach themselves to Hitler's rising star.

He frowned, remembering what he had just seen in the newsreel cinema. It was obvious that the German-made newsreel of the two dictators, embracing each other as if they were age-long friends, wasn't just enemy propaganda. Franco and Hitler would be more than just nomimal allies soon. He'd bet his bottom dollar that Franco would join Hitler to take an active part in the war, and that might well mean there'd be German soldiers strutting down this very street in their heavy jackboots before 1940 was out. It was something he hardly dared think about. The very idea made him feel sick, and he was sick far too often these days.

He went on, scarcely noticing the crowds of servicemen and shabby civilians all around him. A lot of them seemed without a care in the world, young girls laughing; soldiers whistling at them; governesses, pushing their charges in polished prams, complete with crests, making the usual chuckling noises that nurses made. Did they know what it was going to be like when the Germans and their Fascist allies came? London could well be another Barcelona or Valencia, scenes of terrible atrocities and mass death and destruction. How would such careless, unsuspecting people cope with Fascist terror, where a man – or a woman, for that matter – could be shot out of hand for carrying a crucifix or wearing the leather jacket of a worker? Their smiles would be wiped off their faces permanently – those who survived.

Deep in thought, he didn't wait to cross at the Belisha Beacon, named after the War Minister, now sacked, who had boasted the year before that nothing would stop the B.E.F.[*] It was the best equipped army Britain had ever sent overseas. Now it was obvious that army was in total disarray, fleeing before the German attackers. Instead the tall man stepped off the pavement. A horn blared. A Cockney voice bellowed angrily, 'For Chrissake, mate, look where yer bleeding going!' followed by another saying in the arrogant, familiar tones of an old Etonian, 'I say, fellow, can't you look—' the arrogant voice stopped suddenly. It snapped, 'Stop there, cabbie. I want to talk to this gentleman.'

'But I'm in the middle of the traffic—'

But the owner of the voice was not listening. As the cabbie fumed, he stepped out of the taxi, elegant in his tailor-made naval uniform, a cigarette perched in a long ivory holder. 'Hello there. It's Blair, isn't it? Or do you call yourself Orwell all the time these days?'

The emaciated man stared at the lieutenant-commander, his sleeve adorned with the jagged stripes of the 'Wavy Navy', the Royal Navy's wartime auxilliary service. He was languid, with a supercilious, broken-nosed face that would have seemed attractive to some women, probably women as snobbish as he was. But there was something about the naval officer's eyes that would make a more discerning person treat him warily.

They were hard, filled with a barely concealed ruthless look of the kind that some people would describe as belonging to the type of individual who would go over dead bodies to get what they wanted.

He looked at the officer in bewilderment, while other taxis

* British Expeditionary Force.

honked their horns at him and their drivers snorted, 'Get out of the ruddy way, mate, yer holding up the traffic.' Not that the officer noted them, or the fact that the cab's meter was ticking away merrily. 'Do I know you, Commander?' he asked.

'Not me personally, Orwell, but my brother Peter. I think you were at Eton with him before he set off on his deuced gallivanting around the world, supposedly exploring or some such nonsense . . . Frankly I think he just liked wandering about, instead of trying to hold down a decent job in the City.'

Orwell's sunken, worn face lit up. 'Now I know. Peter Fleming . . . You must be his younger brother, Ian.'

'Exactly, old chap. That I am.' Suddenly the naval commander became aware of their position in the street and the minor jam they were causing. 'I say, let me give you a lift. I've always been interested in scribbling a novel myself. Like to pick your brains, what? Buy you a drink at White's, if you like.'

George Orwell, as he was now known in London literary circles, was about to refuse. He had no time for fellow Etonians, especially those like this arrogant bugger, who seemed to think the world was his oyster – which it was, coming as he did from a wealthy Scottish banking family. Then the last newsreel picture he had seen of the two dictators, Franco and Hitler, hugging each other, flashed into his mind, and with it the need to stop them before it was too late. He found himself saying, 'All right, Fleming. Thank you, I will. I rather fancy a stiff drink at this very moment . . .'

Five

The bar at White's was crowded with men, some in civilian clothes but mostly in uniform, and all looking very important. Orwell was of the same class as most of them, he knew, ex-officer, old Etonian and all the rest; yet he took an instinctive dislike to them. They seemed to represent, even now, when they were in uniform and were seemingly going to fight against Fascism at last, a class he detested. To him, they were those who had inherited privileges they had not earned, and had been determined to retain them, come what may, even if it had meant making a pact with the Devil in the shape of those Fascist dictators. The Fascists would do their fighting for them and keep world revolution from their precious 'sceptred isle', as they would have called Britain in their pompous, unthinking fashion.

Even the porters had looked on him in a somewhat supercilious fashion as the two of them had entered the Club – his shabby tweed suit had obviously not gone down well with them. But Fleming's uniform had, and his arrogant manner, as if he not even been aware that they were there, had done the rest.

Now, as they stood at the bar with the red-tabbed staff officers and civilian servants in well-cut black jackets and pinstriped trousers, drinking Bloody Marys, Fleming announced completely out of the blue, 'It's all very hush-hush and all that, Orwell, but I know you're one of us. You'll keep it under your hat, but I'm in Naval Intelligence – that's my boss over there –' He indicated a florid-faced rear admiral, busily engaged in tackling a very large whisky – 'Admiral Godfrey. Good sort, though he didn't go to school, of course. Dartmouth, naturally. Gives me my head, however. We're always on the lookout for . . .'

But Orwell was no longer listening to Fleming. He was considering what the arrogant bugger in his fancy uniform had just said – *Naval Intelligence*. Was it just a coincidence, or was it fate? Wouldn't Naval Intelligence be the starting point for the plan which was beginning to form in his mind, like some deadly snake slowly uncoiling, ready to reveal its fangs? He took another sip at his Bloody Mary, as near to him, one of the red-tabbed army colonels, who sported an old-fashioned monocle, was blustering, 'I say if our chaps over there run away at the first sight of a Hun, they ought to be lined up against the nearest wall and shot out of hand, like we did with rotters of that kind in the last show.'

'You just mentioned Naval Intelligence, Fleming?'

'I did. What of it, Orwell?'

'I'm thinking of something I'd like to suggest to someone in your line of business, Fleming. But–' Orwell shrugged his painfully thin shoulders, a symptom of the disease that would eventually kill him – 'unfortunately I don't know anyone in your business, until, of course, now, when I met you.'

Fleming looked amused, but said merely, 'And what is it you wish to convey to Intelligence, Orwell? You can talk openly here. They're all trustworthy chaps here at White's.'

Orwell took a sip of his drink, wishing it was beer, and told himself he wouldn't trust the present company, with their flushed, well-fed, self-important faces, for a moment. 'Well, Fleming, it is my guess, after being in Spain and fighting the Fascists, that Franco will throw in his lot with Hitler in the end, especially now, when the Germans are winning in France.' Hitler will offer Franco the bribe of Gibraltar, or something like that, and ambitious as he is, Franco will jump at the offer.'

'And we will be in an awful pickle in the Med as a result,' Fleming interjected. He had just remembered his date with a whore, and he didn't want to be late for his twice-weekly afternoon session. It was difficult enough to find educated girls who indulged in his specialist tastes.

'Exactly, Fleming.'

'So what are you suggesting?'

'This. We deal with Franco before he has a chance to do

a deal with Hitler. There are plenty of his generals who would like to take over from him and don't want to involve Spain in yet another war, especially when she is still recovering from the Civil War.'

'You mean – bump him off, Orwell?'

At any other time Orwell would have been amused at Fleming's 'bump him off'. It illustrated the quality of his mind and imagination, obviously nourished by cheap gangster novels. 'Yes, bump him off, Fleming.'

The elegant naval officer considered for a moment or two. The pompous Colonel across the bar was saying loudly 'What our people need is a cavalry just like Haig's in the old war. Horses can run rings around tanks, and a damned good cavalry charge, eight hundred riders armed with sword and lance, going all out, would put the wind up the German infantry. They'd break and run for it as if the Devil himself were after them.'

'Hear, hear,' some of his flushed, tipsy listeners agreed heartily. 'Well said, Bimbo!'

At that moment Orwell felt a little sick. The silly old buggers weren't just fighting the last war; they were bloody fighting the war before that.

Fleming stroked the rim of his glass thoughtfully, as he might one of the cats he doted on. 'It's an interesting idea, Orwell. But there are certain imponderables.'

'There always are in such matters,' Orwell snapped impatiently.

Fleming didn't seem to hear. He continued in a soft voice, almost as if he was talking to himself. 'I mean, although we have diplomatic representation in Spain, it is still a really difficult country to get into. Our diplomats there are limited to certain areas and there are police spies and agents everywhere.' He raised his voice. 'Besides, who could we find who spoke fluent Spanish, that is, probably a Spaniard himself, who would risk his neck going back to his native country? Surely a man like that would be on the police's wanted list.'

'There are refugees enough in this country who might take that risk, Fleming.'

Fleming sneered. 'But they're parlour pinks for the most part, full of self-importance. I can't see that kind of individual risking his neck even if he were capable of carrying out the dirty deed.' He shot a glance at his watch. 'I tell you what, Orwell. I'll discuss it with my boss, the Admiral, and then get back to you.' He gave the other man a fake smile. 'Duty calls, you know.' He nodded to the barman. 'My account, Alf.' He turned back to a sombre Orwell. 'Perhaps we can get together some time, old chap, and discuss the novel. I'm awfully interested in the mechanics of the business. You could give me some tips. Must rush.'

And with that, he was gone, leaving Orwell feeling let down and eager to get out of the bar, which stank of privilege and class distinction, and everything that had made him go to Spain to fight with the International Brigade in the first place . . .

Fleming got out of the taxi at the end of Cheyne Walk. He looked left and right. It was well known that ladies of easy virtue lived in some of the place's elegant flats, and he didn't want some prying Special Branch man spotting him in such surroundings. He'd done well in the 'Wavy Navy' so far, and he didn't want trouble with his boss Admiral Godfrey – although Godfrey wasn't perfect himself. To the horror of his senior Intelligence colleagues, the head of Naval Intelligence kept an enemy alien as his mistress, namely an Austrian woman.

The coast was clear. A little earlier on, the air raid alarm had sounded, and that had helped to empty the streets, though so far there had been no real German aerial attack on the capital. He pressed her bell three times; their usual signal. She answered over the intercom almost immediately. 'Just getting changed for you, darling,' she trilled. 'Found some new black frillies. I'm sure you'll like them. Come right up, darling.'

Fleming needed no urging. He felt the old familiar thickening of his loins.

He was looking forward to what was soon to come, Orwell and his suggestion forgotten for the time being.

Mrs Divine Bottom, as she called herself on her calling

cards – she swore that it was her true name – was waiting for him, already dressed by now, or it would be better to say undressed. She was a plump woman in her late thirties, with a creamy white skin that had never seen the sun, it appeared; it was set off perfectly by her black leather boots and skimpy French lace knickers.

'Darling,' she gushed, and handed him a Martini even before he asked for one. As always, she was very liberal with the drinks he paid for and which she offered, he suspected, to her other 'gentlemen', as she called them. He didn't mind. Her type of prostitute, and the expertise she had built up over the years she had been 'in the business', were very hard to find.

'Drink and ogle,' she urged, and twirled her body round, bending down so that he got the full benefit of her ample bottom, covered in the thin black lace. 'Now, isn't that a pretty picture to set a naughty man's heart racing, eh?'

He choked a little on his Martini and nodded his agreement, taking in those delicious rounded globes and dark crevice.

'You look absolutely adorable,' he said thickly, 'a real dish, as the Yanks say.'

She winked knowingly. 'I bet you can't wait to get at it, eh, Commander? You military gentlemen are always so fierce when it comes to punishing us poor wicked women.' She fluttered her false eyelashes and looked over at the walls of her drawing room, where hung, what she called 'the tools of the trade': sticks, whips, riding crops and the like. 'I expect you're impatient to get down to business immediately.' She twirled round once again, and, bending, exposed her buttocks, which she then wiggled provocatively.

He swallowed hard. 'Can I use the riding crop? It goes with the boots.'

'Of course, my darling,' she simpered. 'After all, that's what I am here for – to give my beloved pleasure.'

Fleming licked his lips, which were suddenly very dry, and reached for the riding crop. He flexed its supple length. She shivered dramatically and pleaded, hands clasped together in the classic pose of supplication, 'Please, master, don't hurt me too much . . . *please*.'

It was all part of the ritual, and Fleming was intelligent enough to understand that. But it was a necessary ritual: one that he had to believe in and follow scrupulously if he were going to enjoy the pleasure that the whipping would give him. 'It depends just how naughty you have been,' he hissed threateningly, and swished the rising crop through the air. She trembled, as he expected her to do.

'I confess that I have been naughty. I've been thinking sexy thoughts, master.'

'I see,' he replied grimly, face stern. 'Then you must be punished. Kiss the whip, wench . . . D'you hear, kiss the whip *at once* – or it will be the worse for you.'

She did so humbly, gaze fixed on the ground like some schoolgirl confronted by a severe headmaster. He licked his lips again. He liked that. He felt a great surge of power, dominance, sweep through him as he commanded hastily, 'Take those knickers off immediately, or else.'

Hurriedly, as if terrified, she slipped out of the black panties.

'Over the edge of the couch.'

She did as she was ordered, crying piteously, 'Please . . . please, master, don't be so cru—' She yelped as he brought the lash down on her naked behind, his sense of dominance growing apace as a sudden red weal sprang up from that smooth, pearly-white flesh. The ritual was well underway . . .

It was later, as she snuggled her head between his naked legs, completing the session in the manner that he expected from her, soothed now and relieved of all tension, that it came to him.

He had the power – he had just proven that – power to do anything, even if it was perverted and illegal, if he exerted himself. That Red Orwell had suggested an attempt should be made on Franco's life. It would be discounted immediately in official Whitehall circles. Hadn't both Hitler and the new premier, Churchill, agreed that there should be no attempt made on the lives of enemy politicians? But what if a bold man like himself, who didn't care for convention, worked out a plan and carried it out successfully; what could those bowler-hatted bureaucrats do then? They couldn't bring

Franco back to life. Besides, if by such a bold stroke he could keep Spain out of the war, a major piece of *realpolitik*, he'd be famous. The state would, in due course when the stink blew away, heap on rewards.

Even as she started to call a cab for him his mind was racing electrically, trying to work out a rough-and-ready plan of assassination . . .

Six

'*This is the drill!*' the young Highlander officer bellowed. He needed to. The noise on the coast just outside St Valery, where the survivors of the beaten 51st Highland Division were trapped, was tremendous. Down below the cliff on the beach, littered with dead Scots and broken boats, the white-capped sea raged. All around, the panzers of General Rommel's 'Ghost Division' pounded away, ensuring that sooner or later, the division, minus its artillery, would have to surrender soon; above, the massed squadrons of Stuka dive-bombers circled and circled like predatory hawks waiting for the opening to come howling down in their lethal dives, sirens shrieking, ready to unload their cargo of destruction on the defenceless Scots.

'We light the smoke bombs. Once they start to smoke and form a screen, you're up on your feet and running all-out. Once you're through the smokescreen, you're down the cliff the best you can. No freezing. With a bit of luck – and you'll need it by God,' he added under his breath – 'the boats from the destroyers over there'll take you off and you'll be having eggs and bacon back in Blighty before you can say Jack Robinson . . . Clear?'

'Clear,' the men lying in the parched cropped grass answered without too much enthusiasm. They'd already seen half a dozen of their comrades emerge from the protective smokescreen to go over the edge of the cliff in their haste, screaming wildly, arms flailing as they fell to their deaths. It was clear, too, that some of the Royal Navy's heavier war ships had given them up, already beginning to head for 'Blighty', a dark smudge on the other side of the Channel. Still, most of them were prepared to have a go.

They didn't want to spend the rest of the war in a German prison cage.

Cusi, who had listened carefully to the young Highlander's instructions, now translated them into Catalan for the benefit of his men as they waited their turn to run the gauntlet of German fire.

The men of the 51st Highland Division had been good to them. They had fed and re-armed them and seen the Catalans through the bloody fighting against the Germans until they had reached the coast and could go no further. His experienced eye told him that those who were going to get away would be those who made the attempt now, before darkness fell. Soon the Germans would wait no longer. The advantages were all on their side. The British were trapped with their backs to the sea. They were running out of food, water and ammunition, and their casualties were mounting rapidly. The Highlanders wouldn't last much longer, and Cusi knew what his and his men's fates would be then. Foreigners in British uniform, who had once fought Franco and had attempted to destroy the *Deutschland*: their German captors wouldn't waste much time on them. They'd be put up against the nearest wall and shot in cold blood. He and his men *had* to escape. The alternative was death.

Cusi, crouched in the second line, waiting to rush the clifftop through the smokescreen, being ignited again by the Division's sappers, watched as the first line, commanded by an elderly, white-haired staff colonel with a brick-red face, who looked as if he might have a heart attack at any moment, prepared for the ordeal. Most of them had slung their rifles; a few had apparently flung them away, a bad sign. But all were tense, leaning forward like greyhounds waiting for the signal to break from their traps.

The officer raised his hand. He hesitated momentarily. Then he blew a shrill blast on his whistle and yelled above the angry crack of small arms, '*GO! . . . GO, LADS!*'

The old colonel flung a look behind him. It was, Cusi thought, a mixture of anger, despair and shame. It was clear that the Englishman hated himself for abandoning his comrades in this manner. But at the same time, he knew he had to do it. There was no hope left here. The Germans had them trapped. They could hold on a little longer, but in the end, they would suffer the ignominy of surrender, and that would mean years of imprisonment behind barbed wire.

The colonel made up his mind. Already the much younger men were racing ahead, vanishing into the smokescreen, while the German fire intensified, the tracer bullets hissing through the grey smoke in a kind of glowing white, lethal Morse. He ran into the fog.

Cusi shouted above the racket, 'Spread out, comrades. If anyone's hit, keep on running. Go over the cliff. Better a broken bone than a Fascist firing squad.'

Cusi's Catalan veterans spread out, leaving large gaps between each escapee. Cusi pulled out the big British service revolver he had taken from one of the dead officers, who lay sprawled out everywhere on the clifftop. Behind him came the wail of those strange pipes that these Scottish-Englishmen were so fond of. He nodded his approval. They were showing a brave face in this moment of ultimate despair, now that it was almost over and they realized that long years of imprisonment lay before them: young men who might be old before they returned to their wild, remote country. For an instant, he was reminded of their own position and their homeland, and wondered when they might ever see it again. Then a young officer was bellowing, as the Stuka dive-bombers started to fall out of the sky to bomb the few remaining little boats off the bottom of the cliff, '*GO, LADS* . . . *G—*' His order ended in a strangled cry of pain. Through the wavering smoke, rising thickly now, Cusi caught one last glimpse of him as he fought gamely to remain on his feet. To no avail. With one last desparate cry, he fell and vanished from their view.

Cusi and his Catalans went off out. Bullets cut the air to left and right of them, ploughing up the turf in vicious little spurts of green and brown. The escapers didn't seem to notice. They ran furiously, arms working back and forth like pistons. Jordi was hit. He stumbled and, vaguely glimpsing him through the grey smoke, a horrified Cusi thought the 'holy man' might fall. But Jordi recovered just in time and staggered on.

84

Now they were coming to the edge of the smokescreen. The stiff breeze coming from the sea beyond was blowing it rapidly. Cusi coughed and tried to clear his lungs of the damned smoke. Down below, the group before them was wading furiously through the white, raging surf. In some cases they were tossing away their weapons in their panic. Further out, the remaining destroyers were being bracketed by the German guns inland. Huge geysers of water spouted all around them. Indeed, one of the British ships had been hit and was listing badly, trailing thick black smoke as it started to make its escape before the enemy brought the full weight of their fire to bear on the stricken ship. Cusi realized that time was running out fast. If they didn't get to the destroyers soon, the destroyers would be gone; they wouldn't risk being sunk much longer for the sake of a handful of disorganized riflemen.

He sprang over the cliff top. He slithered down in a mini-avalanche of stones and turf. To left and right, his men were doing the same. Halfway down Cusi braked. Some ten metres ahead there was what seemed to be a sheer drop leading to the beach, already littered with the dead and the moaning Highlanders who had broken a limb going down. His heart missed a beat. To the right, sneaking carefully around the rocks, there were men in those familiar, hated coal-scuttle helmets. Fritzes! They had sneaked a patrol down to the beach somehow or other. Soon they'd set up the machine gun they were carrying, and that would be that. They'd slaughter the escapees mercilessly. Cusi tightened his grip on the big .38, grateful that it was attached to his upper body by the loop running around his neck.

Now, instead of attempting to work his way round the sheer drop, he began to move sidewards, coming in above the still-unsuspecting Germans, crawling from one tuft of grass to another, careless about making any noise, for the thunder of the German guns would drown any he might make.

The German patrols had found a suitable spot at the edge of the barnacle-clad rocks. The gunner and his mate slapped down the air-cooled Schmeisser and started feeding in the long belts of gleaming ammunition which would allow the gun to fire nearly a thousand rounds a minute. They were smiling, Cusi saw, as he got ever closer to them. '*Bastards*,' Cusi whispered beneath his breath. He clutched the revolver in a hand that was wet with sweat. '*Tally-ho!*' He used his mother's favourite expression in English. Next moment he launched himself into space, firing as he did so from the hip. At that range he couldn't miss. The fat German bringing up more belts of ammunition fell immediately, what looked like a steaming grey snake emerging slowly from his shattered stomach.

The gunner's mate tried to make a run for it. He didn't get far. He yelled as Cusi's second slug tore his kneecap off. For a moment or two he tried to hop on. He couldn't. He pitched forward into the sand, turning it a dark red immediately with his own lifeblood.

The gunner tried to roll round, heaving the machine gun with him. It was obvious he had already spotted from which direction the attack had come. He was going to bring up his 'Hitler's saw', as the German soldiers called the high-speed weapon. He didn't get a chance. Cusi shot him between the shoulders. He yelled piteously, but kept his finger on the Spandau's trigger. Even as he died, he kept firing purposelessly on the air before finally, with a kind of apologetic stutter, he stopped, and there was silence.

Cusi had no time to exult in his little victory. Already one of the last of the Royal Navy rowing boats was approaching the beach of death. A naval officer in a blue helmet and carrying a megaphone was calling very calmly, 'Please hurry this way, gentlemen . . . In an orderly fashion . . . If you try to rush the boat, I shall be forced to fire . . .' Then, in an attempt at humour, perhaps to calm what was obviously a very tense situation with more and more Germans advancing down the beach to cut off the escape, he added, 'This way for the *Skylark* free trip round the bay . . . sick bags provided . . . This way for the *Skylark* . . .'

Cusi's English was good, but not that good. He didn't understand the business of the *Skylark*, but he did know that it meant hope, and a chance to get out of this mess to fight against the Fascists on another day. 'Line up,' he commanded, 'and do what the officer says.' Cusi knew his Catalans; they had no sense of order and habit of standing in line, as the English did even in such desperate situations as this.

The young officer in the blue helmet looked momentarily puzzled. Then he decided that the foreign tongue must be French. He said, '*Parlez-vous français?*' Why, Cusi never could understand afterwards: Why should he ask a soldier he thought was French if he spoke his native language, French. But, as he reasoned to himself, 'the English were always very strange.'

Now, however, there was no time to account for the strange customs of the English. Hastily they were bundled into the rowing boat, with the wounded Jordi crossing himself and repeating his prayers as if his very life depended upon it, until one of the sailors, a hoary old petty officer, said, 'No use going on about it, chum. A couple of hours from now you'll be drinking a pint of wallop in some snug. This will be just a sweet dream.'

And that was that, and so they sailed for England with the survivors packing the deck of the overloaded destroyer, drinking mugs of cocoa laced with rum, half drunk with the spirits and relief, bellowing away at the tune of that summer, '*Roll out the barrel . . . We'll have a barrel of fun . . . Zing, boom, tararel . . . we'll soon have old Hitler on the run . . .*'

Cusi frowned momentarily. He wondered. They would not have 'old Hitler on the run' this year, or the next for that matter. Then he dismissed the gloomy thought and stared at the growing blob of white and brown which was England, and wondered what lay ahead for them there . . .

Seven

'Fleming – Commander Fleming?'

Commander Fleming took his eyes off the nubile young Wren who was kneeling in front of his fire, navy-blue skirt hitched to reveal a delightful stretch of firm white flesh above her black, non-regulation silk stocking. She was new, but willing. How willing he didn't know, but she was pretty, and somehow she had wangled him a bucketful of precious coal for the fire, although it was only June. But then he always liked a fire even in summer, especially in the bare, large Admiral room which was the centre of Naval Intelligence. Reluctantly he took his gaze off the naked flesh. 'Yes, Fleming here,' he said in his best languid old-Etonian manner.

'It's Orwell,' the voice said at the end of the phone.

For a moment Fleming looked puzzled. 'Orwell?' he echoed.

'Yes, George Orwell.'

'Oh yes. What can I do for you?' Fleming said without interest. From what he had learned since he had first met Orwell the previous month, he had discovered that the writer was something of a class traitor. Old Etonian as Orwell was, he had betrayed his class by consorting with working people, and worse, actually joining left-wing parties, intent, it appeared, on closing public schools, including their *alma mater*.

'Can I have a few minutes of your time, Fleming?'

Fleming was inclined to say no, He wanted to talk to the young Wren, to check if she might be a suitable person for one of his many seductions. But already she was rising to her feet, blowing on the coal dust sticking to her hands. That

88

delightful stretch of stocking and naked flesh was disappearing. 'All right, what is it?'

'It's a recording one of our people took at Hastings the day before yesterday. I think it might interest you. It's one of a group of survivors from France just being landed there by your navy chaps.'

'Recording? Must I?'

But Orwell still had retained some of his Eton arrogance. For he said with sudden determination in his thin voice, the product of the TB which one day would kill him, 'Yes.'

Fleming cursed, but smiled winningly as the Wren said, 'Thank you, sir,' and went to the door with the empty Ministry of Works coal bucket. 'Thank you, Wren,' he said warmly. It was not often that he acknowleged the effort of other ranks. It wasn't the done thing for the officer class. Still, the girl had potential. He wanted to get on her best side, other rank or not.

There was a click, as if someone had switched on a gramophone, a whirr, and then a flood of words from an excited voice. Behind it, there was the background of ships' sirens and the stamp of heavy boots marching in unison. 'The great rescue of the BEF and their Belgian and French comrades goes on. Last night to the shores of Britain came thousands more men who only a few hours before had been fighting in Flanders and other parts of France.

'In all the tremendous drama of the last week or so, the eyes and hearts of Britain have been with the fighting men doggedly facing the German hordes, with the RAF and the Royal Navy whose deadly shelling and bombing have given them respite to reach our coast. But I want—'

'What the devil is this nonsense?' Fleming exploded. 'Why are you wasting my precious time with this propaganda? After all it's all a load of rubbish, everyone knows we were defeated, the Huns are running us out of France. Don't you know there's a bloody war on?'

Orwell kept his temper. He knew he had to. 'Bear with me a few more moments, Fleming, and listen carefully.'

'For what?'

But Orwell did not seem to hear. Instead he turned up the

volume of the BBC recording. Now the sound of marching feet had died away, as had the customary hooting of the ships' horns, as if Britain had just won a great victory and it needed to be celebrated in the traditional Navy fashion.

'Now I want to tell,' the enthusiastic commentator continued, 'of the unsung heroes of this great enterprise. I mean the fishermen of England who bravely and selflessly answered the call to save our soldiers. For the strange new armada which made the rescue possible is what I call "the Fisherman's Armada"—' Orwell stopped the recording abruptly and said sharply, 'Did you hear it, Fleming?'

'Did I bloody well hear *what*?'

'The music.'

'No, I did not. Now, Orwell, what's the game? What are you wasting my time like this for, eh?'

Orwell responded by repeating the same bit of commentary, and now an angry Fleming could definitely hear a strange wailing pipe music in the background. To him it sounded like some bloody animal being slowly strangled to death.

'Now do you hear it?'

'Yes, I ruddy well did, Orwell . . . So what?'

'Do you know what that music is, Fleming?'

'No, I don't bloody well want to. Now will you get off this bloody line, or shall I contact the authorities and have you arrested for wasting a government official's time?'

Orwell didn't seem impressed by the threat. Instead he said, a note of quiet triumph in his voice, 'There's the men you want.'

'Want for what, damn you, must you speak in riddles?'

'You remember that thing.' Now Orwell was cautious. Perhaps Intelligence people's phones were tapped as the Communists had done in Barcelona, when they had virtually taken over in that beleaguered city back in '38.

'What thing?'

'About Spain and the – er – General. You must remember, Fleming. What the fat pig might do when Hitler finishes off France, which he will do soon?'

Fleming's anger vanished immediately. He recalled that conversation the two disparate old Etonians had held in the bar at White's the previous month. 'Yes, I remember now. Go on, Orwell.'

'You talked about the difficulties in finding someone who could carry out the nasty business.'

'Yes.'

'Well, I think we might have found that person or persons, Fleming.'

'How do you mean?'

Orwell didn't answer his question. Instead he said, 'I think it's better we meet privately to discuss the matter. We *scribblers* can't afford the White's Bar. But I do know a quiet little pub off Bloomsbury called the Oporto.' He rubbed it in happily. 'Very working class, you know, whippets and cloth caps sort of thing.'

Fleming didn't rise to the bait. He was too eager to find out what Orwell had discovered. 'Suits me, I'll dress down. When?'

'Saturday night. Nobody goes out on Saturday nights any more in case the Germans start bombing. The place will be half empty.'

'Agreed.'

'See you then, *Commander* Fleming.' The phone went dead, leaving Fleming sitting there hunched in the battered old Ministry of Works' chair, wondering what the connection was between that strange, tortured, wailing pipe music and the proposed assassination of the Spanish dictator . . .

'Bloomsbury,' Orwell announced as he and Fleming were assailed by the thick blue fug of cheap tobacco and stale beer.

'Bloomsbury,' Fleming echoed, nose wrinkled in disgust. 'Smells more like a cheap East End dosshouse to me.'

Orwell allowed himself a slightly malicious smile. What would Fleming know about cheap dosshouses? He'd wager that the commander, who was wearing what he probably thought were cheap casual clothes – a well-cut tweed jacket and flannels that were creased to perfection by some batman or other – had never slept on a flea-ridden mattress that stank of old man's piss in his life.

91

A few casuals hunched over their beer, making it last, stared at them as they entered, and then went back to their dominoes and reading of the *Daily Mirror* once more.

Orwell led the way to the bar. The Cockney behind it, Woodbine tucked behind his right ear, seemed to know the BBC writer. 'Hullo, Mr Orwell,' he said familiarly, 'what's yer tipple tonight? We've got some bottled ale under the counter,' he lowered his voice, 'for special customers.'

'That'd do fine, Alf,' Orwell said. He turned to Fleming, who was dusting the dirty bar stool with a fine linen handkerchief anxiously, as if he were afraid if he didn't he might catch some terrible disease. 'What about you, Fleming? What would you like to drink?'

Fleming asked hesitantly, 'Do they have Scotch in places like this Orwell, a double if they do?'

'God bless yer, sir. Course we does. Look over there.' Alf pointed to a lone black bottle with a white label up on the top shelf, out of the reach of thieving fingers. 'Don't be vague, ask for Haig, as the slogan goes, sir.'

'Yes, Haig will do. Plenty of ice, not much water.' He looked at the filthy water jug on the beer-washed counter. 'In fact, I don't think I'll have any water at all.'

Together they moved with their drinks to the far end of the long, narrow bar where the light was dimmest and the newspaper readers and domino players wouldn't settle down on account of the lack of light. Orwell took a drink of the warm ale straight from the bottle, and Fleming shuddered slightly at the thought of a fellow Etonian sinking so low. Orwell coughed and said, 'All right, Fleming. I'll put you out of your misery. You want to know what I meant over the phone, don't you?'

Fleming nodded numbly.

'It's this. I didn't notice the first time I heard the recording. But I heard it again and then I noticed. There was the sound of pipes, and people dancing in the background.'

'Dancing!'

'Yes, and it wasn't the Scots doing the Highland reel, I can assure you. Indeed, the only time I've heard that kind of dance music,' Orwell gave a wary grin, 'was in Spain, in Catalonia, to be specific, when we were retreating from the

Fascists. That was back in the winter of last year.'

Fleming looked totally puzzled. But Orwell wasn't going to enlighten him just yet. Indeed, he took pleasure in stringing the supercilious bugger along. Besides, despite Fleming being in intelligence, he doubted whether his fellow old Etonian even knew where Catalonia was. So he continued with, 'It's a kind of folk dance native to that part of Spain, and I probably don't have to tell you that during the Civil War, Catalonia was the last part of Spain to hold out against Franco to the very end, with what was left of its troops going into French exile rather than live in Spain under the Fascists.'

Hastily Fleming grunted, 'Yes, yes of course.' He took a quick sip of his Scotch to cover his embarrassment. 'But where is all this leading, Orwell?'

'To this,' Orwell said, a note of triumph in his weak voice. 'What are Catalans doing landing with the remnants of the Highland Division at Newhaven? . . . Further, of what use could they be to you and your plan?'

Now he took a long drink of his ale, savouring the other man's bewilderment.

'I still don't understand,' Fleming admitted finally.

'Well, this is what I think, Fleming. If these Catalans were evacuated with the Scots, it must mean they fought on their side. From that, I conclude that these Catalans must be soldiers who fought against Franco, somehow got to France and then were prepared to fight on on our side. If that is the case, I put this to you.' He lowered his voice significantly. 'Would they be prepared to go a step further and – er – deal with Franco? They know the country, they are native speakers, and once we – you – got them to Spain, say by submarine and plane, they'd blend in easily. And remember, there must be hundreds of thousands, millions of people in that country who could well be prepared to help them. They would be perfect tools for the job, and remember, they wouldn't be doing it for fame or money, but from a burning desire to free their homeland from—'

Orwell never finished his passionate declaration. For in that instant, the pub's blackout curtain was ripped aside and a loud drunken voice cried, 'Make way for a hero, gents . . . A veteran of Dunkirk.' An undersized soldier, cap bearing the badge of the Army Pay Corps, tunic ripped open, burst into the snug, face flushed with alcohol, pointing a shaking finger at the brand-new patch attached to his right shoulder. It read 'Dunkirk Survivor'. It was almost as if the drunken Pay Corps clerk thought it signified some great immortal battle honour.

Brushing by the old men playing dominoes and knocking their counters to the sawdust, he swayed and staggered to the bar, where Alf was waiting, a little open-mouthed at this strange apparition. 'Get me a drink, a big drink, barman – drinks for the house.' He waved his hands wildly, almost falling over with the effort. '*For free*,' he added. 'Nothing's too good for our boys who fought at Dunkirk, eh?'

Alf wasn't impressed. 'No tickee, no washee, as the Chink says, mate.' He tried to sound humorous, but Orwell noted the sudden hard look in his eyes. Alf had seen it all before.

'You can't talk to me like—' The drunk never finished his protest. With surprising agility for a man of his age, Alf had sprung over the bar, grabbed the drunk by his jacket collar and the seat of his pants and had propelled him through the door into the blackout outside before the old men playing dominoes had really become aware of what was happening.

He clapped his big hands together, as if he were wiping something very dirty from them, saying, 'It's all right, gents. Just another of those drunken sods who think we'll win the frigging war by running away.' A moment later, he was slumped behind his bar again, busily engaged in reading the sports page of the *Daily Herald*.

Fleming looked at Orwell. 'You say find these Catalans, Orwell. But how can we when the army's spread all over the show, with five thousand deserters on the run and London full of stupid soldiers like that? Discipline and order have gone to pieces. If the Hun comes, most of the conscripts'll be like that awful individual: they'll get drunk, desert their regiments and go back to mother. How can we find anyone under those circumstances?' He looked hard at his fellow old Etonian, and at that moment, Orwell had no answer to that overwhelming question . . .

BOOK THREE

To Fight Again

One

Commander Fleming was right.

The British Expeditionary Force, which was thrown out of France by the victorious Germans that summer of 1940, was in total chaos. Twelve to thirteen divisions had fled back to Britain. They had gone to the Continent as organized, cohesive bodies of men, each division numbering up to eighteen thousand soldiers. Now they had returned in bits and pieces, separated from the divisions, frontline infantry that had done the fighting mixed up with the rear echelons, dental troops, HQ clerks and the like, who had been told to drop what they were doing to 'get the hell to the coast – *anywhere* where there'll be boats to take you back to Blighty'.

Tank divisions had gone back without a single tank. The artillery had blown up or abandoned their guns. Even the infantry had only been able to save their personal weapons, their rifles and revolvers. And back in England, there was only sufficient equipment available to re-arm a single infantry division.

That summer Anthony Eden, the new War Secretary, had journeyed secretly to York to meet his top generals. His mood was grim that June. Meeting his generals, all veterans of the trenches in the First World War like himself, his mood grew even grimmer. They pulled no punches. They told the handsome Minister that if – and when – the Germans invaded Britain, the Regular Army could be counted on to fight, even if they were evacuated to Canada, to which the King and Queen and the Royal princesses would be sent. Not the conscripts. They'd go home to their loved ones and there wait and see what life was like under the German occupiers.

Already five thousand men who had returned from Dunkirk had 'gone on the trot', as the soldiers called desertion.

The result was that divisions were split up, not even the divisional commanders knowing where all their men were. Now the only priority that the hard-pressed, still shocked staffs could give themselves was to get as many soldiers, whatever their arm of the service and regardless of any formation they had once belonged to before Dunkirk, to the coasts of the British Isles. Here they were set to work digging beach defences against the supposed German invaders soon to come, while the Government tried to buy basic arms, rifles, revolvers, mortars and the like from the still neutral Americans.

No one was exempt from this almost panic-stricken levée, even foreigners. Anyone who wore some sort of military uniform and seemed ready to fight for Britain was pressed into service. Thus it was that Cusi and his Catalans, still dazed by their transition from France to England, where everything appeared totally different from what they had been used to all their lives – why, the English even drove on the wrong side of the road – were assembled in a great sprawling camp outside London that first week of June. Here, surrounded by weary soldiers speaking, it seemed, half a dozen languages, even German, they were addressed by a colonel standing on a podium, who, despite his immaculate gleaming pre-war uniform, looked perplexed and ill at ease.

Through his megaphone, he had cried, 'I shall speak to you in English in the hope that you will understand. I shall speak slowly and carefully. Now please pay attention.'

The Czech and Poles, still in French uniform, looked at each other in bewilderment. The German-Austrian Jews who fought with the Pioneer Corps – 'the shit and shovel brigade', as the infantry had called them contemptuously – understood all right, but they looked even more worried than ever as the middle-aged colonel in his shining boots and elegant white riding breeches commenced his address. After all, if the Germans did come, they would be the first to be shot, as Jews and traitors. Cusi's Catalans, fishermen from the little villages of the Costa Brava for the most part, simply stood there stoically and waited without understanding a word.

'I will not attempt to minimize the situation,' the officer cried, as over London to the south, the sirens started to sound the alarm: the German bombers were coming. 'We are in a mess. We have few weapons. We have to maintain the defence of a long coastline, and we haven't enough soldiers to do so.' There was a sudden note almost of despair in his voice, and abruptly Cusi recalled the one-armed General Cugat making similar desperate appeals in what now seemed another age. His heart went out to the Englishman, who under other circumstances he might well have thought of as a hidebound old fool. 'It is for that reason I am here today,' the colonel continued. 'I want to ask you men if you will volunteer to take an active part in the defence of England and fight, if necessary, the Hun.' Hastily, almost as if he didn't want them to think too closely about what he had just said, he went on: 'I know you all face special difficulties, more than our own English soldiers. But I feel it is in your own interests to continue the fight.' He shook his head and lowered his megaphone momentarily, as if he were suddenly aware of what desperate straits the country found itself in, having to appeal to foreigners, many of whom didn't even speak English, in this manner. He pulled himself together rapidly, however, and snapped in the style of a senior officer used to giving commands and having them obeyed, 'Those who are prepared to do their duty and fight on, take one pace forward – MARCH!'

For one long moment nothing happened. Then in close formation, the Poles, and after them the Czechs, stepped smartly forward. The Jews of the Pioneer Corps, who had never learned the British Army's three-hundred-year-old drill followed more awkwardly. Cusi swung his head round to look at the French, who made up the biggest contingent. But they were not moving. A few of their officers in the traditional *kepi* were whispering at them, obviously urging them to step forward. But the rank-and-file were not moving. They were remaining stubbornly where they were, some shaking their heads vehemently, a few openly mouthing their reluctance. '*Non . . . pas du tout!*'

Suddenly Cusi was angered by the sight. He remembered their own treatment by the French military when they had sailed the battered *Vittorio* into the harbour at Nîmes, and what had happened thereafter. He looked at his Catalans, who hadn't understood a word of what was going on. '*Val*,' he snapped in Catalan and took a smart pace forward, as if he were back in his prewar cadet school.

Bewildered as they were, his volunteers didn't hesitate. Where Cusi went, they went. One day later they were all members of the British Army, dressed in a smelly new battle dress, wearing great clod-hoppers of the new steel-shod Army boots and on their way in a blacked-out express heading north to some remote English province called Yorkshire . . .

Reluctantly Fleming took his eyes off the little Wren's provocative bottom as she knelt in front of the fireplace, placing pieces of coal in the grate, balancing them carefully on the wooden sticks. Every time she moved, she exposed more of that splendid white thigh, drawing her skirt more tightly over the outline of her knees. In his mind's eye he visualized himself slipping them down to reveal the tight round globes of flesh beneath. But now, as he heard that heavy stomp coming down the corridor towards Room 40, he dismissed such lascivious thoughts. It was the Admiral outside, stamping along as if he were still on the quarter-deck of the cruiser he had once commanded. 'Wren Smithers – *Ann*,' he allowed himself her first name, though he didn't approve of such familiarity between officers and other ranks on duty, 'think you'd better stop. It's the chief, Admiral Godfrey.'

She blushed at the use of her first name. 'I could always come back, sir. I always like to have the fire ready in case you need it.'

'Very good of you, Wren. But I'll be OK.'

He caught one last glimpse of her thigh as she rose hastily in the same instant that the Chief of Naval Intelligence flung open the door, as if he might well pull it off its hinges, and barked, 'Morning, Fleming . . . Morning, Wren.' As usual, he whipped off his gold-braided cap, threw it at the hatstand

and, as usual, missed. 'Blast,' he snorted. 'In the old days I always managed it—' He stopped short as the young Wren bent down to pick up his cap and hang it on the hatstand. He winked at Fleming as her skirt rode up again to reveal those sheer silk stockings and the metal catches of her suspender belt, but he waited till she was gone with her coal bucket over her arm like a shopping basket, before saying, 'Fine young filly, that, Fleming. Pity she's another rank.'

'Sir,' Fleming dutifully replied.

'Now, Ian,' when they were alone, he always used his subordinate's first name – 'What's with this Spanish business? You know the thing that that bolshy Orwell from the BBC mentioned?'

Fleming looked glum. 'Not really much further, sir, I am afraid. I contacted one of the Highland Division people – most of them are in the bag now.'

'Yes, bloody bad show. A fine division like that surrendering to the Hun. No matter. What did he say?'

'He confirmed that there were some sort of Spaniards brought back with the last boats to escape from St Valery. I suppose those Spaniards are Orwell's bloody Catalans.'

'And?'

'That's about as far as I've got, sir. What's left of the Highland Division is being sent or has already gone back to Scotland to recruit and reform. But as far as my informant could say, these Spanish chaps didn't go with them.'

'So where did they go? Even in the mess we're in at the moment, no one in his right mind would leave a bunch of armed foreigners running around like that. God knows what they could get up to. Bad enough with so many of our own chaps deserted and on the run from the police. There are break-ins and burglaries all over London at the moment. Remember, we've already had trouble with the Frogs who won't fight on in Portsmouth? We've had to send in the Marines to deal with them. They just want to go back to their own country and sit out the rest of the war on their Froggie arses. So these Spanish greasers of yours will have to be somewhere controlled by the brown jobs,' he meant the British Army. 'They've got no homeland to go back to.'

Fleming nodded his head, a little miserably. Admiral Godfrey was not the brightest of officers; he was more at home on a warship than in an office. He needed Fleming to come up with the ideas that he could later claim as his own and justify his position as head of Naval Intelligence until he could escape back to sea.

'Look at it like this, Ian. These Spaniards are dependent on us for bed and board. They are not enemy aliens who Churchill is currently consigning to internment on the Isle of Man. "Collar the lot", he's ordered. So where are we keeping them?'

Fleming realized the Admiral had hit the nail on the head this time. 'Of course, you're right, sir. I'll get on to it straight away.'

'Do that, Ian.' The Admiral rose to go to his own office, where he studied the latest edition of *Jane's Fighting Ships* for most of the time, preparing for the happy day when he returned to sea and the real war, and not this bloody 'war in the shadows', as his subordinate, with his penchant for the melodramatic, always called the Intelligence conflict. 'One thing, however, Ian, at this juncture.'

'Sir?'

'How are you going to make these Catalans carry out the dirty work when and if you find them—'

Suddenly the phone on Fleming's desk began to jingle. He cursed. 'Excuse me a moment, sir,' he said.

The Admiral nodded and wondered yet again how he was going to spend the long day ahead of him. *Jane's* was very interesting, but ship recognition, tonnage and displacement became pretty boring after a while. Perhaps he might indulge in a long watery lunch before going and paying a short, but exciting, visit to Trudi, his Austrian mistress.

'Yes?' Fleming snapped.

'It's Orwell . . . George Orwell,' the voice at the other end said. The Red scribbler sounded very excited for some reason or other.

'Yes, what can I do for you, Orwell?'

'I've got some news for you.'

'Have you?' Fleming retorted without enthusiasm.

'Yes, it's about our Catalans.'

Fleming sat up. 'Fire away, Orwell.'

'Well, a chap in our World Service, you know, the BBC—'

'Yes, I know what the World Service is, Orwell. Get on with it, man.'

'Well, he was telling me in the BBC canteen about the strange requests his people get from all over the place. Even here in the UK there are so many foreigners now that they're bombarded with requests for foreign languages. Why the other day . . .'

Fleming pulled a face at the Admiral, who was now deep in thought about Trudi's speciality, which not many English girls, even prostitutes, were prepared to do, even for a fiver. Indeed, he often thought that Trudi enjoyed doing it to him. Afterwards she always joked 'Well, Geoff, it does mean that you don't have to put on one of those rubber things of yours. What you call them – Spanish letters?'

'Anyway, the World Service bloke told me that only the other day they received a request to play songs in Catalan on their Spanish service. More importantly for us,' – Orwell paused as if he knew he was about to deliver an important punch-line – 'could they include a recording of the *Sadana*!'

'What?' Fleming exclaimed.

The Admiral sitting opposite was so startled that all the thoughts of Trudi vanished from his head in a flash. 'I say, Ian,' he snorted, 'what the devil's going on, eh?'

But Fleming was so excited by Orwell's news that he had no time for the Admiral at that moment. 'Did your chap get an address for the man who sent in the request for this sardine thing whatever it's called?'

'Yes and no.'

'What do you damn well mean, yes and no?'

'Well, no address for me. But perhaps one for you.'

Fleming flushed angrily. 'For God's sake, Orwell, don't give me any bloody riddles. I have no patience for them. Cough it up.'

'My chap received an Army Post Office Number, which doesn't give me any clue where these Catalans might be based. All it tells me is that they're with the British Army, and if that's the case, you ought to be able to find it out. After all, you are in Intelligence, aren't you, Fleming?' But as always, irony was wasted on Fleming. 'Right,' he snapped, 'I'll be right over to Broadcasting House to collect that address.' Without even wasting time to give his informant a grudging thank you, Fleming slammed down the phone and picked up his cap to face a puzzled Admiral Godfrey. 'You asked, sir, what would I do if these Catalans were not prepared to carry out the mission we've discussed?'

Godfrey nodded.

'Easy, sir, I'd ensure that they would be returned to their native country as undesirable aliens, and then inform the Spanish Legation here in London what I was going to do.' Fleming allowed himself a wintry smile. 'I don't need to draw a picture of what would happen to them when they arrived in Spain, do I, sir?' He stretched out his elegant, manicured finger and peered along it with one eye closed, as if he were looking through the sight of a rifle. '*Bing!* And that would be the end of those damned Reds. Mention that possibility to our reluctant heroes and I'm sure I could convince where their true duty lay.' He plonked his cap on his sleeked black hair at a jaunty angle, obviously very pleased with himself.

Then he was gone in a hurry, leaving the Admiral to stare at his empty seat, mouth sagging open stupidly, as if he could not quite believe what he had just heard.

Two

It all started during the great storm of that summer of defeat. It was as if the very sea was determined to wipe this stubborn little island off the coast of German-held Europe off the map. Great angry rollers swept in time and time again. The wind lashed the trees dotted along the shore, uprooted them with its elemental force, felling great oaks, snapping off branches like thin matchwood. Lightening slashed the sky in jagged zig-zags of violet light. All was noise, destruction and primeval fury.

Everywhere the gangs of Irish navvies working flat-out on double-time building beach defences, and the engineers blowing great holes in proms, in the seaside resorts to make way for the machine gun and artillery pits, downed tools and fled the cold pouring rain for shelter. Even the soldiers guarding them and waiting for the first Germans to appear, for everyone knew that Hitler was about to launch his Invasion of this last bastion of defiance to his domination of Europe, sought cover, their greatcoats and capes dripping wet, contraceptives stuck absurdly on the muzzles of their rifles to keep the moisture out.

Grimly, however, Colonel Tidmus-McLeod, formerly of the 51st Highland Division, stuck to his 'post', as he called it to his daughter Annabel. Hour after hour, his food served to him on a tray by his former batman, ex-Corporal Egan, he sat on a riding saddle in the great French window, staring out at the storm-tossed North Sea through his telescope. On his left, there was his old twelve-bore; to his right, his service revolver, which the War Department had allowed him to keep after he had been compulsorily retired (more than once, he had told himself that the authorities probably hoped that he

105

might shoot himself and solve the problem he presented that way) loaded and ready, with a spare box of ammo at its side.

For the disgraced Colonel wanted the Germans to come. Then he could die fighting, as he had always expected he would, and his name would be cleared. If the Huns didn't, he hardly knew what he would do. After he had deserted his men at St Valery – and he had come to accept the fact that he *had* deserted them – he had been retired with unseemly haste; his wife had fled the shame to the family estate in the wilds of Scotland, and he had been left here on the East Yorkshire side of the Humber Estuary in the run-down country house, left to him by one of his many aged aunts, attended only by his daughter Annabel and Egan. It was a lonely life. But it was the kind of life he sought now. He didn't want people of his own class, especially if they were in uniform, who might ask him what he was doing here, a regular soldier of these last thirty years, who had fought in France, the North-West Frontier, Iraq and the like, when the Army was crying out for experienced officers. Once a silly young clerk from Beverly masquerading as an officer had come to the lonely coastal house to enquire whether he had any firearms, and whether he and Egan were prepared to join something called the 'Local Defence Volunteers' newly formed by 'Mister Eden'. At the moment all he could offer in the way of uniform, the 'counter-jumper' had explained, was an armband bearing the initials 'LDV', but Beverly HQ expected uniforms to come in any day now, and with a 'bit of luck, sir, I might be able to get you a commission and a company.' He had beamed winningly at the red-faced colonel in disgrace.

Egan had seen the clerk off within five minutes. 'Ruddy Look, Duck and Vanish, sir,' he had said somewhat indignantly afterwards. 'Dinna you idiot ken that we belong to the Royal Scots?'

'Did, Egan . . . *did*,' the Colonel had said somewhat sadly, and, glad the counter-jumper had gone, returned to his telescope on its tripod to search for the Germans ready to invade the Humber and the death in action that he sought now.

But even Colonel Tidmus-McLeod realized on the day of the great storm that the Hun wouldn't be coming this day.

The weather was just too bad for an invasion. Still, he stuck to his post. Twice Egan came in and reported, 'Fire lit in the drawing room, sir. Be warmer there, sir.' and 'I can serve luncheon in the kitchen, sir. Warm as toast in the kitchen, sir. Perhaps a wee dram afterwards, sir.' But both times he had refused, although the thought of that whisky, for a man who had always loved his 'wee dram', had been very tempting.

Instead he had continued to peer through the telescope, swinging the tripod from side to side at regular intervals to survey what he could see of the beach and the furious, raging North Sea beyond. But about midday, when even he was beginning to tell himself that he was wasting his time, his attention was caught by a small group of men, some with rifles slung, butt upwards over their shoulders, others, who were obviously civilians, with potato sacks over their heads to protect themselves against the beating rain, trudging miserably into the grounds of his house, obviously heading for the shelter of his gazebo and the big neglected greenhouses.

'I say,' he barked, talking to himself in the manner of lonely men. 'What the devil do they think they are about—'

'Think they're about what, Daddy?' a voice broke in.

It was Annabel, his daughter, clad in an old-fashioned long riding habit, which had probably belonged to one of his long-dead aunts: it looked positively Victorian. Despite the weather, Annabel was obviously going to canter her horse along the sands. Like all girls of her age, his daughter was mad about horses.

'You ought to be at school again,' he snapped, though his eyes were suddenly warm as he remembered that she and Egan were the only two who had stood by him since St Valery.

'I'm an evacuee, Daddy,' she answered and patted his white head. 'Besides, I've got to look after you with Egan.'

'Evacuee – *from Scarborough!*' He looked at the grounds again. The strangers, sheltered now by the ruins of the old greenhouses, were urinating against the wall, steam rising from the urine in the cold of the day. 'My God, what kind of British soldiers are those? Urinating in front of a young girl. This is not wog country! This is Britain.'

She laughed easily, as if she saw men urinating in public every day. 'But they're not British soldiers, Daddy.'

'Well, what kind of damned soldiers are they, girl?'

'They could be anything. You don't go out Daddy. If you did, you'd find this stretch of coast is full of foreigners. Irish and Welsh labourers and soldiers mostly from the Pioneer Corps, who speak all sorts of languages.'

'The shit and shovel brigade, ah,' Colonel Tidmus-McLeod sniffed contemptuously. 'One can expect anything from that type, if you'll excuse my French, Annabel.'

'I will, Daddy,' she replied. 'But then I'm used to you swearing.'

'All the same, Pioneer Corps or not, I'm not going to have them doing that sort of thing on my grounds.'

'Do you want me to go and choke them off, as they say here in Yorkshire?'

He frowned. 'I don't know so much, Annabel. They are foreigners, you know. Types like that are capable of anything.' He looked up at his daughter from his saddle, as if he were seeing her for the first time; and in a way, he was. For he realized that since he had gone to France the previous year, glad to be on active service once more and full of high hopes for his military future, his daughter had changed. She was no longer the puppy-fat schoolgirl in the straw bonnet and wrinkled black stockings. She was a woman now, with her mother's figure, full-breasted and slim-waisted, with a head ablaze with the same reddish hair that had been his when he had been younger. At sixteen, he realized on that stormy day, she was a desirable woman that men would lust for, and one who, too, would be very vulnerable in the clutches of some unscrupulous older man. He had to watch her and make sure that she didn't make the kind of silly romantic mistake that might ruin her future life. 'All right,' he said finally. 'Just see 'em off. Threaten them with the law if necessary, if there's any law left in our poor old country, and remember, I'll be watching you all the time through my scope.'

'Don't worry Daddy,' she laughed and planted a loving

kiss on his worried forehead. 'I can take care of myself. Ta-ta for now. ITMA, you know!'

He shook his head and told himself that despite the fact she had the body of a fully grown woman, she was still a child, the way she picked up these new-fangled phrases from the bloody wireless.

It was thus that Annabel Tidmus-McLeod met Acting Corporal Angles Cusi of the Pioneer Corps, as he would soon introduce himself to her, for the first time, and start the ball rolling which would lead to his arrest and subsequent recruitment into the plot to kill 'the Frog', otherwise known as General Franco, *Caudillo de Partido Falange de Espana* . . .

'But he's a really nice man, Mr Egan,' she protested to a granite-faced ex-batman as they sat together drinking cocoa (his doctored, naturally, with a hefty shot of the Colonel's single-malt as was usual) a few days later, with the sun streaming through the dirty, cracked French window. 'He's half English, you know. His parents, including his English mother, were murdered a couple of years back in their Civil War. He wouldn't tell me much about it, but it must have been pretty horrible. Can I have some more cocoa, please. It's really sweet.'

'They do a lot o' funny things in them foreign places, ye knew, Miss Annabel,' the Colonel's batman said seriously, pouring her another mug of the precious cocoa, obtained on the Bridlington black market behind the railway station in exchange for one of the Colonel's bottles of vintage sherry, which the hard-drinking ex-Royal Scots considered a drink fit only for 'silly old dames and tarts'. 'And remember, he's half a foreigner hissen.'

She sipped the fresh cup of cocoa, savouring its taste after a week without sweets (she'd gobbled her ration up within twenty-four hours of receiving it) and forgot Mr Egan for a few moments, savouring the thoughts of that handsome young man with his blond hair, ready smile and easy, confident manner. She knew her father had never considered the 'other ranks', as he called them, really full human beings. For him, private soldiers were there to be looked after and treated like grown-up children who respected their military elders, until the time came for them to carry out his orders and go dutifully to their deaths. But her 'Angel', as she called Corporal Angles Cusi, was different. He knew so many things that she didn't – he had even been forced to show her where he came from on the map of Spain in her school atlas – and he treated her like a real woman, and not as a child like her father and Mr Egan. Why, at their first meeting, as she prepared to give him a good talking-to, he had interrupted by asking her what her first name was. Surprised, she told him.

Drenched as he was by the pelting rain, he'd looked up at her on her horse and said, '*Annabel* . . . oh, my beautiful Anna.' For a moment, she had thought that he'd follow the transformation of her name, which she really didn't like overmuch, with a kiss on her hand, in the manner of the Poles who were supposed to do it all the time. Angles didn't; she'd learn later that the somewhat dour Catalans were not given to kissing women's hands. All the same, his charm had won her over, and instead of the stern lecture she had been prepared to give him to appease her father, she had compromised with, 'I hope you'll look after the place? My father's pretty strict about such matters. Thank you.' With that, she had turned the mare and trotted back down the drive to the house, forcing herself not to look back at him. But when she had succumbed, he had been still standing there in the pouring rain, staring. She had blushed for the first time since she had been a spotty third former back at school in Scarborough.

She had seen him several times since then. Every now and again he gave her what he called 'little gifts', not that they were the kind of presents a man was supposed to give to a woman he was trying to charm. Once it was a bar of army ration chocolate, what he called his 'iron ration', slab of bitter dark chocolate in a brass tin. Another time it had been a case of flashlight batteries to be used in the blackout, taken from a freighter torpedoed and beached just off the mouth of the Humber. Then there had been the half a dozen codling which one of Angles's soldiers had caught off the beach when he had been off duty. Egan had been delighted with the young, very fresh fish. 'They're no the herring, mind ye,

Miss Annabel,' he had lectured her. 'But yon fish is no bad. The colonel'll be muckle pleased to have 'em for his supper tonight. Take his mind off things.'

The Colonel had been 'muckle pleased' that same night. Indeed, he did forget his shame and his telescope for a while as he ate two of the fish which Egan had prepared for him, using the whole of his own butter ration to fry them.

But afterwards, as he enjoyed the sensation of having eaten well and the rare treat of good fish, savouring the single malt, he had looked at Annabel, who was pleased with her father and was delaying her nightly visit to Angles so that she could share the old man's rare happiness, and had asked casually, 'Where in heaven's name did Egan get such good fish, Annabel? I thought the Hun had put a stop to most of the coastal fishing. They say the Hun are attacking even simple fishing smacks these days.'

The question had caught her completely off guard. She had blustered something about a local man coming to the door and selling the fish to Egan for a shilling. But even as she made up the story, she had realized that her father knew she was lying. He, like she, knew that ordinary civilians were no longer to go on the beach, which, now that the Irish navvies were finished with their pillboxes, had been turned into minefields, marked by wooden boards headed with a skull-and-crossbones above the legend 'DANGER! MINES. FORBIDDEN TO CIVILIANS!'

Colonel Tidmus-McLeod had said nothing. But that evening after he returned to his study and his telescope, he told himself that now not only had he to watch out for the Hun, but also his own daughter . . .

Three

The great storm that had raged that June brought in its aftermath several surprises to that north-eastern coast, most of them unpleasant. As the tides abated and the water returned to its normal summer's gentle swell, the soft lap-lap of the sea against the shore, the soldiers of the Pioneer Corps repairing the damaged beach defences discovered the dead bodies of those poor unfortunates of the Merchant Marine torpedoed off the mouth of the Humber, just when they were within sight of Hull and safety. Not only the bodies of men, but those too of poor animals, cows and sheep and the like, trapped for ever in their wooden cages, perhaps still alive when they had floated out of great jagged holes made by the German torpedoes, to be mauled and eaten alive by marauding fish now patrolling the mouth of the estuary, eager for this new source of food provided by the Germans.

But for Acting Corporal Angles Cusi of the Pioneer Corps now in charge of a sector stretching from Spurn Point almost to the old run-down resort town of Withernsea, the aftermath of the great June storm brought with it a surprise which, for a change, was relatively pleasant.

It was an upturned fishing smack which had obviously been under the water for a long time, perhaps even sunk before the war. For its timbers were worn smooth by the action of the water and the shingle, and there was little trace of its crew save for rusty candle-holders and a tarnished compass, dated '1905'. And for once there were no water-logged bodies, human or animal, in its wrecked interior.

Cusi said nothing of his find to the others. Instead, he borrowed a mine-detector from one of the hard-pressed sappers, working all-out to find out whether the storm had

112

displaced the beach minefield, and set about working a mine-free path to the wrecked fishing smack, resting on its side, half buried in sand at the bottom of the muddy cliffs, which were a feature of that part of the desolate coast with not a house within miles.

What mines he found – and there were very few of them – he dealt with quickly, using the techniques he had seen the sappers use: a quick feel around the deadly packet of high explosive to check whether it was attached to another by a thin, almost invisible piece of wire; a cautious grope beneath it, fingers tingling and feeling red-hot he pushed them through the sand and underneath the mine to ascertain whether some evil-minded sapper had placed a matchbox fuse there which would go off and explode the mine once some over-eager soldier tried to raise it without checking for such a devilish device.

Panting a little, as if he had run a race, and sweating hard, he had cleared and marked a path to the wrecked boat, and then returned to the cliff to re-erect the warning board with its skull and crossbones and the chill message: 'MINES'.

It was here that he and his 'Anna the Beautiful' began to meet. She would ride out from the big house some five miles away, tether her mare on the top of the cliff, and with his help descend the muddy ground and follow the marked path cleared of mines to the overturned fishing smack. Inside, he had arranged an old mattress taken from the houses further inland, which had been compulsorily evacuated by the military, and a small spirit stove on which he would cook the rice pudding and other delicacies he had filched from the Pioneers' cookhouse at the Point.

Here, with the sea beating on the shore ten yards away, the water slithering back and forth on the shingle, they would eat the strange food (at least for him) and sip the too-sweet tea, which again he disliked, and talk and talk. He would tell her of his youth, the war, how both his parents had been shot out of hand by Franco's men in Madrid at the beginning of the Civil War just because they had been overheard speaking Catalan together instead of Castilian in the centre of the capital. She would listen, and gush with almost girlish

113

enthusiasm about her horses, the girls at school, and her desire to grow up quickly, till at the age of eighteen she would be old enough 'to do something exciting before the war's over,' and she would 'have to get married to some local chap with money and breed.'

He would smile, amused at her expressions and enthusiasms, and realize again that the real war was so far away from her life in this provincial backwater that she was totally unable to comprehend the bloody realities of battle. It was better thus, he told himself. In war, young people grew up too quickly; they saw things they wouldn't be able to wipe from their memories even if they lived to be a hundred years old.

So he dropped his native seriousness and humoured her, enjoying doing so too. For her, these secret meetings when he cooked those dreadful English dishes in the cover of the boat, which smelled of seaweed and diesel oil, were like picnics, or those secret candlelit 'dorm feasts', as she called them, whatever they were. It was the thrill of the forbidden. Cusi reasoned that she'd never been alone with a grown man nearly a decade older than she was, who had sexual desires and wishes that she had never even dreamed of.

Occasionally he had forgotten that she was so innocent; the sex drive had been too strong for him. He had pulled her towards him and felt her breasts pressed against his battle dress blouse. She hadn't objected. Instead, she had closed her eyes, as if she were expected to do so, while he had tried to restrain himself, his nostrils full of the delightful smell of woman mingled with that of some inexpensive scent, and had pressed his mouth hard against hers. Time and time again he had tried to press his tongue in between her lips, only to meet the barrier of her teeth, as if she couldn't understand what he was about. But afterwards she would breathe dreamily, while he worried about his bulging loins and the fact he felt he must burst with repressed sexual passion. 'Oh darling, you make me so happy, the way you kiss.' And then she might well say, 'Angel, do you think I might have what's left of the rice pud in the pan? It's ever so nice and sweet.'

On the last day of June 1940, however, the daily secret

tryst appeared to be spoiled by the change in the weather. She was late for the rendezvous, explaining as she hurried down the treacherous mud cliff, 'Daddy was awkward, in one of his black moods, I'm afraid, asking me why I was going out when a sea fret is on its way.'

He hadn't known exactly what a 'sea fret' was but he guessed it meant the damp fog which was curling in from the sea like a grey, silent cat.

'I had to wait till Mr Egan pacified him with a large Scotch – Daddy's drinking far too much these days – telling him the Germans wouldn't invade today. The weather would be too bad.' She had shivered, and instinctively he had taken her in his arms and led her protectively to the shelter of the boat, outside of which he had lit a fire from the wood which lay everywhere on that beach of wrecked and battle-shattered boats.

Later, he thought she had exaggerated the cold, pressing herself against him so hard that he couldn't help touching those splendid breasts of hers, as if she had something else in her mind than just keeping warm in the damp, chill fog. Indeed, later he concluded, as she mentioned more than once that 'Daddy' was getting suspicious of her daily rides, and had suggested she ought to return to school and prepare for her Higher School Certificate, whatever that was, or take a job in nearby Beverly or Bridlington, that 'Anna the Beautiful' had come to some sort of crucial decision.

As that afternoon dragged on with the sound of ship foghorns out to sea muted by the fog, and there came a steady drip-drip of moisture dropping into the fire and making the logs splutter and spark, it was clear that she had. She even turned down the offer of that heavily sugared rice pudding she usually delighted in, saying, 'I don't feel like it today, dear Angel . . .' She had lowered her eyes demurely for a moment. 'I've got other things on my mind.'

Gently he had tilted her face up, saying, 'What sort of things?'

She had steadfastly refused to meet his gaze, whispering hoarsely, 'I don't know how to tell you, darling.'

'In words,' he had joked.

115

The joke failed. She had responded with, 'Words are not much use. It's feelings that count now.' Idly (or so it had seemed then) she had dropped her hand on to his lap, and he had been both shocked and suddenly very excited, as if he had discovered something about Annabel he had not known before.

'What kind of feelings?' he had asked, trying to control himself.

Then it had all come out in a rush, while her hand seized his penis and squeezed it hard in the manner of an innocent who was trying to give him pleasure, not knowing that even the toughest-looking man needed to be treated gently down there. 'I want to be grown up at last . . . I can't wait any longer . . . Everyone is at war, doing things, experiencing things, doing *that* . . . Me, I'm still a silly schoolgirl . . . playing with horses . . . Angles,' she had raised her head then, her dark eyes full of passion, 'I want to live – and love . . .'

On the cliff-top, Mr Egan, shivering in the damp fog that shrouded his skinny frame so that he looked like some spectre standing there in that empty wildness, had seen enough. Too much, in a way. Now he was torn between his loyalty to the Colonel, who had sent him cycling through the fog on this spying mission, and young Miss Annabel, who he had known since she'd been a little girl, who if he had not been a confirmed bachelor, he would have loved to have had as his own daughter.

What was he to do? He turned, not wanting to hear the noises that he knew so well from army brothels all the way from Bombay to Boulogne and which told him all he needed to know, as sad as it was. Slowly, he started to ride back to the big house.

Thirty minutes later he was there. He paused, panting a little from the exertion, his face damp with the fog, as if covered with sweat, and stared at the big French window of the Colonel's study which overlooked the sea. As always, the old man was sitting there in his hunting saddle, weapons to left and right of him, poised at the telescope which seemed these days to be his only link with the real world outside.

He stared at the man he served so long, and wished for a

116

moment that they had never attempted to break out throughout that cliff-top smokescreen at St Valery. It would have been better for both of them if they had died then, as both of them had expected to ever since they had become soldiers so long before, weapons in hand, blood racing with the desperate fury of battle. Instead, they were condemned to this: an existence rooted in a momentary aberration of judgement and a suspicion now of the real world outside their purposeless existence.

Suddenly he made up his mind. He gave the bike a hefty, angry push like he might have done some stubborn 'beast' of his Highland farming youth. He went inside the house. He removed his gumboots and padded silently in his stockinged feet to where the old man kept his precious malt. He poured himself a very large glass. This time he didn't even bother to add water to the decanter to cover the theft.

For what seemed a long while, he sat there, lost in thought, the fog-muted silence broken only by the foghorns out at sea. He rose and decided he had to get on with it. But his courage failed him again. Instead, he poured himself another glass of the whisky. This one, however, he drank more swiftly, as if he knew he had to be drunk before he approached the old man. His mind raced. It was filled with rapidly moving pictures of the past, like some cinema newsreel speeded up for brevity's sake: the Royal Scots in Hong Kong, all spats, kilts and solar toppees; the old man as a company commander sporting his new Military Cross in Palestine, telling the men, stood at ease, that they had really won the medal for bravery, not he; that awful day at St Valery when the division collapsed and the old man made that overwhelming decision which had ruined him . . . He stopped and stood up, a little unsteadily now. 'Corporal Egan,' he commanded himself, 'git on parade.' He straightened his shoulders and drained the last of his stolen Scotch. He opened the door, and then set off down the corridor to the old man's study with that bow-legged swagger of the regular Scottish infantryman, who had once belonged to 'Pontius Pilate's Bodyguard', the oldest regiment in the whole of the British Army.

He paused at the door. He swallowed his spit in the hope that it might hide the reek of the whisky – it didn't.

117

'Come,' the old man called.

He entered and stamped down his foot as he were reporting to the Orderly Room, back in what now seemed another world. 'Sir,' he barked.

Colonel Tidmus-McLeod turned from gazing at the fogbound sea, and said without interest, his mind far away on other things, 'What is it, Egan?'

Egan hesitated. He hated to say what he had to say now. 'It's Miss Annabel, sir.'

The old man shook his head like a man finding it difficult to wake up from a heavy sleep. 'What is it? Have you found—'

Egan was so eager to get what he knew off his chest and free himself from the stigma of what he regarded as a betrayal, that for the first time since he had served with the old man, he interrupted the Colonel. 'Sir, I have to report that Miss Annabel . . .' Outside the grey mass of the damp fog was split suddenly by a jagged arrow of bright light, followed by the hollow boom of steel striking steel: a U-boat had torpedoed yet another ship as she slowed down to enter the Humber Estuary. Neither of the two old soldiers seemed to notice.

Four

It was Friday again, the high point of the week for most of the Royal Engineers and their supposed comrades of the much-maligned 'shit and shovel brigade'. It was payday.

Now in the bright midday sunshine (the sea fret had vanished at last, heralding the happy weekend to come, perhaps), they lined up in their various formations, the Sappers well spruced up and their brass polished, for no one wanted trouble on this special day; the Pioneers sloppy and unmilitary as always, though they had polished their boots and tried to adjust their forage caps to the right regulation angle.

They stood in lines of three, the men positioned in alphabetical order, each one carrying his paybook inside his 'AB64', ready to hand over to the paying-out officer. In front of them there was a trestle table, covered with a grey army blanket, complete with inkwell and wooden army-issue pen. Behind, there were two collapsible wooden chairs, guarded by the Sapper's staff sergeant who would be in charge of the payday ceremony, a borrowed pacing stick under his arm, which he handled as if he might be a frightening drill sergeant in the Brigade of Guards. Every so often, he would glare at the men of Cusi's 'shit and shovel' group and bellow, 'And remember this, you greasers – when the paying-out officer calls yer name, march straight to the table, salute, whip off yer beret, get yer pay, hat on, salute and turn smartly to yer frigging left and march off. Bags o' bleeding swank. Get it?' And he would point the brass-shod pacing stick at them, as if he were considering whether or not to run it through them there and then, before dropping to murmur; 'Bloody shower o' shit!'

Cusi smiled. He was used to British Army NCOs by now. They were full of what they called, when they were drunk in their messes, 'piss and vinegar'. They didn't mean most of what they said – it was part of the drill – and even if they did, his Catalans certainly wouldn't understand.

At precisely eleven hundred hours, the little utility van, driven by the pay sergeant, with the paying-out officer of the Army Pay Corps sitting next to him, arrived for the weekly ritual. This time the van was accompanied by a truck with a military policeman driving it, which caused the waiting sappers to murmur among themselves. 'The frigging Redcaps – somebody's for the high jump, mates. Anyone forged his paybook?'

But already the Royal Engineers' staff sergeant was calling the pay parade to attention, and the waiting men had no time to eye the two Redcaps, who had emerged from the back of the Bedford truck, pulling at their immaculate trousers and adjusting their pistol belts, complete with leather-holstered .38 revolvers.

The bigger of the two was a staff sergeant. He had a friendly sort of face – for a military policeman. But then, he was no wartime recruit: the medal ribbons and the golden stripe on his sleeve indicated that. He had a look about him that said he knew his squaddies – he'd seen it all before and would probably see it all again before he retired. His companion, with the bright new white stripe of a lance corporal beneath the military policeman brassard, was a different type altogether. He was younger, and very definitely keener. He had one of those sharp faces that any real military criminal, or even one who was merely a suspect, would find unnerving. His eyes seemed to bore into men of the pay parade assembled before him as if he suspected that each and every one of them was up to no good.

The big, slow-moving staff sergeant appeared to feel the same about his subordinate, for he said, 'Remember, Barney, we're not here to arrest the bloody lot of them.' He smiled, rolling his Rs in the fashion of a countryman of his native Gloucester, as he went on to say, 'We're here to pinch the bloke in the front of the foreigners, and we don't want no trouble with them – there're too many for us, Barney.' His tone changed as the Sapper sergeant stood the pay parade at ease. 'All right, Lance Corporal, eyes to yer front. Here we go.'

The ritual commenced. One after another, the sappers had their names called. They snapped to attention, marched stiffly to the trestle where the two Pay Corps men waited, saluted and removed their caps, waited to be given their thirty shillings weekly pay, placed the note and the coins in their caps and departed as stiffly as they had come, their minds probably full of how many pints of 'wallop' the money would buy before it ran out.

Now it was the turn of the Pioneer Corps men.

Standing to the side, Staff Sergeant Wheatley nudged his subordinate. 'Here we go, Corporal. Now remember, take it easy.'

The Engineer Staff Sergeant looked at the Pioneer Corps' nominal roll, licked his lips as he prepared to shout out their damned greaser names, and began with '*Corporal Cusi, A!*'

By now Angles knew the drill well. Indeed, he liked it. It reminded him of his days as a naval cadet before the war, when everything had been discipline and order, instead of his wartime service with the Republican Forces, which had really been an armed, ill-disciplined mob. He stepped forward smartly and marched to the table. But already he sensed that something was wrong. The fussy Pay Corps officer with the tortoise-shell spectacles had suddenly appeared not to be interested in the cashbox which contained the men's pay. Instead, he fumbled nervously with his wooden pen, while at his side, the sergeant had pushed his chair back as if he were going to leave at any moment.

An instant later, Corporal Cusi found out his suspicions were correct; there was something wrong, very wrong indeed. As he reached the table, two large men stepped from behind it. It was the two Redcaps. The taller of the two said in a very formal voice, 'Corporal Cusi of the Pioneer Corps?'

'Yes,' he answered, puzzled, wondering what the Redcaps wanted from him.

'I am here to arrest you.' Wheatley nodded to his subordinate without taking his gaze off a suddenly ashen-faced Cusi for a moment. Behind him, Barney Cooper fumbled in his back pocket for the handcuffs.

'For what?' Cusi managed to gasp.

'You are charged,' the big Redcap said even more formally, 'with having unlawful sexual intercourse with a girl under the official age of consent . . . Now, Barney.'

The corporal was very swift. Even before Cusi was aware of what was happening, he had twisted the Catalan's hands behind his back and clicked on the cuffs. 'Done, Sarge!' he reported, proud of his swiftness, it seemed.

The Redcap didn't acknowledge the report. Instead, he kept his gaze fixed firmly on the other Catalans. For a few moments they were too surprised to react. But then Indiano, always the most aggressive of that little band of exiles yelled, 'What are they doing?' He waved his fist at the big MP and shouted in his newly-acquired broken English, 'What you do with my corporal?'

Wheatley dropped his hand to his leather pistol holster significantly. But he didn't draw out the .38. Instead he said calmly, as he had done before to similar hotheads, 'Now, just keep quiet, chum . . . and nothing will happen . . . It's just routine,' he added, voice lower than ever. It was the old trick to soothe the mob: they had to strain to hear. It was no use indulging in a slanging match and shouting back, he had learned that long ago.

'*Pero*,' Indiano began, but the Pay Corps officer snapped, deciding that it was time to assert his authority as the only officer on parade this Friday, 'Steady in the ranks there. I'll never get through paying you, if you bloody well go on like this, you know.'

'Thank you, sir,' the MP said formally, though he knew the Pay Corps type would be the first to fill his pants if things got out of hand. He looked at Cusi, and though he was some sort of a 'greaser' (though he didn't look it with his blond hair), he felt sorry for him. There was something about Cusi's face that made him, the old sweat, sense he knew that he was being set up.

Staff-Sergeant Wheatley nodded to the corporal. 'All right,

Barney, I'm going to turn my back on 'em now and march him off. Just keep behind me and keep yer eyes on him. I don't think they'll try anything.'

'They are foreigners after all,' the keen-eyed young policeman agreed, as if the fact that they were foreigners explained everything. 'Stick a knife in yer as soon as yer back's turned.'

Wheatley snapped, 'All right, son.' He tugged at the cuffs attached to his own wrist. 'Come on now. We don't want no trouble, do we?'

Cusi was too bewildered to reply. He knew he shouldn't have given in to the girl, but she had pleaded so strongly with him it had hardly seemed the moment to ask her age.

Now the three of them backed off, with Lance-Corporal Cooper throwing glances over his shoulder, hand touching his pistol holster, which he had opened, just in case.

Behind them they left the Catalans, their fists clasped in impotent rage, supervised by the officer with tortoise-shell glasses, who felt he was fully in control, not realizing that he and his tin box with the soldiers' pay could be overrun at any moment . . .

Up in his study, the tears pouring down his worn old face, the colonel watched the threesome's progress to their truck. Behind, Egan, equally upset, waited with the old man's tumbler of Scotch, though this day the latter seemingly didn't need his favourite tipple, so in the end Egan drained the glass himself. Still, the colonel didn't notice. And above them in the tiny room into which the colonel had ordered her in disgrace until he decided what to do with her, Annabel Tidmus-McLeod watched the arrest of her one-time lover stony-faced and apparently without emotion.

For this day she realized, with the overwhelming surety of a revelation, that the world was unfeeling, even downright cruel, and that there was going to be no happy future for her as was often depicted in the novels of romance and love that she had been addicted to reading hitherto. She would go through life, year in, year out doing what was expected of her, marrying and bearing children, but she was certain that even the children as yet unborn would never really bring her happiness. She would re-live this moment and what had led up to it this summer of 1940 for the rest of her days.

An hour later the Redcaps' truck pulled up at the little LNER station at Beverly. Staff-Sergeant Wheatley undid the hand-cuff attaching their prisoner to him and rubbed the stiffness from his wrist, while Cusi stood there numbly and Corporal Cooper watched, a little surprised. All around them the passengers laden with their suitcases and kitbags surged by them, heading for the Hull–King's Cross train. A few looked at the prisoner curiously – a couple of tipsy sailors said cheerily, 'Cheer up, mate, it may never happen,' – but the great majority looked away as if they were embarrassed at the sight of a fellow human being chained like this.

Then the older staff-sergeant did something which caught both the aggressive corporal and a miserable Cusi completely off guard. He took his key and undid the prisoner's hand-cuffs. 'Hey, Staff,' Cooper exclaimed, 'what's the lark? Why you letting him go like that? He could do a bunk.'

The staff sergeant smiled and tapped the side of his big nose knowingly. 'You'll find out in half a mo, Corp. Just hold yer horses, that's all, and follow yours truly. All right, Corporal Cusi, move it, will you. There's somebody waiting for you at the London train, chum.'

They moved on with the big staff sergeant leading the way happily, as if he were relieved that all had gone off so smoothly, whatever *it* was. 'First class,' he directed. 'Officers and gents allus travel first class.'

They pushed their way to the front of the train, where the engine was already wreathed in steam and making shuddering noises like a live thing, impatient to be off and start its long journey to London.

Suddenly two figures emerged from the steam: one was tall and elegant in well-fitting naval uniform; the other was a civilian, smoking a cheap Woodbine, his tweed jacket shabby and his flannels baggy and stained here and there, as if he habitually dropped his food on them.

Staff Sergeant Wheatley clicked to attention and raised his

right hand in a perfect salute, while the other two stared at the strangers as if they were alien creatures just deposited here at the small provincial station from Mars. 'Corporal Cusi, sir,' the Redcap snapped. 'As requested.'

Casually, the naval officer raised his gloved hand to his cap. 'Thank you, Sergeant.' His broken-nosed face revealed nothing, though he did fumble with his expensive-looking leather wallet and, taking out two crisp, brand-new pound notes, handed them to a suddenly beaming Wheatley. 'A little gratuity. Get yourself and the corporal a drink. But keep your mouth shut, remember.'

'Thank you, sir. Good of you, sir,' Wheatley snapped. Well versed as he was in the ways of posh officers such as this haughty-looking snob of a naval commander, he asked no more, though in reality he told himself that something strange, even fishy, was going on. Why did they have to arrest the foreigner like this, and why were they being bribed to keep their mouths shut? For what purpose? He contented himself with asking, 'Anything else you need us for now, sir?' Behind him the guard was waving his green flag and preparing to blow his whistle. Couples were giving each other hasty last hugs; children were beginning to cry and yell, 'Bye, Daddy'; the police on duty, checking leave passes and on the lookout for deserters, were marching away from their post at the ticket barrier, heading for 'a char and a wad' in the RTO's office. It was a typical wartime station scene with men off to war, not knowing if they would ever return, and their womenfolk wondering, cheeks wet with tears, how they were going to cope now that their men were leaving.

But the two Redcaps, who had seen it all often enough before, had other things in mind as the shabby civilian with the Woodbine glued to his bottom lip started to talk earnestly to a puzzled Cusi in what Wheatley thought was a foreign language, but which one he couldn't be sure; he thought it might be 'Eyetie'.

'Shall we have a wet, Sarge?' Cooper asked, eyeing the two pound notes in the NCO's big hand.

Wheatley beamed down at him. 'Corporal, we shall have *several* wets, and if we can find a pub where they have some

125

black market bacon, I'm gonna have mesen a big bacon sandwich – and not that bloody stale cheese and onions.' But it was only later, when Staff Sergeant Wheatley was wolfing down his special treat, the bacon sandwich, that the full strangeness of the day's events struck him.

They'd been told that the foreign corporal of the 'shit and shovel' brigade had committed some sort of an offence against a young girl. But that should have been a matter for the civvie police, not the Army. He reasoned that the Redcaps had been called in, probably by the civvie and the la-di-da naval officer, because they didn't want a scene with the Corporal's countrymen, whoever they were. The business with the seventeen-year-old girl had been only a cover to get Cusi from under and deliver him to the station into the custody of the two of them. But why? What was going on?

Cooper seemed to be able to read his thoughts, for he said, wiping the beer foam from his mouth with the back of his hand, 'What do you make of it, Sarge? I mean, all that malarky?'

By way of a reply, the big NCO tapped the side of his nose, as if he knew things that could not be revealed to mere acting corporals, saying, 'Don't ask no questions, Cooper, and yer won't be told no lies. Now drink yer beer like a good little corporal, and if yer behave yersen, I'll buy yer another half . . .'

BOOK FOUR

A Murder is Proposed

One

'At the command of three,' Tiny, their instructor, yelled above the roar of the wind and crash of the waves against the base of the cliff, 'the grapnel will be fired. Then you will move. Understand? Move up the cliff.' It was clear that he still remembered how he had trained the local Chinese for entry into the Shanghai Police; his words were clear and simple, as they should be, instructing as he was Cusi's Catalans. 'Now then, ready. One . . . two . . . three . . . *MOVE!*'

Jordi crossed himself; since they had come to this remote training ground, he had become more religious than ever, even trying to find a Catholic church so that he could go to confession. Hastily, as the grapnel snaked upwards, trailing the commando rope behind it, he leaned forward to take it. Next moment, with Tiny shouting encouragement, he and the rest were squirming upwards, knees gripping the rope as they had been taught, heading for the cliff-top and what lay waiting for them up there.

From his vantage point there, the newly promoted Second Lieutenant Angles Cusi watched their progress with satisfaction. His Catalans had been tough men from the start, but Tiny, who seemed nearly two metres tall, and his fellow instructors from Tenth (International) Commando, which trained refugees and anti-Nazis from half a dozen countries, had made Cusi's volunteers even tougher.

Up to meeting Tiny, the ex-Shanghai Police unarmed combat expert, he had never realized that there were so many ways to kill or disable a fellow human being. As Tiny was wont to begin his lectures to the trainees with, 'It's kill or be killed, men – never forget that,'; and then the big man with the Chinese dragon tattoos and shaven bullet head would demonstrate yet another means of putting an opponent 'out', as he called it. 'Twist their bollocks,' the lecture would go, 'gouge out his peepers, stick yer fingers up his nostrils and tip upwards, clap on both sides of the neck, and if he doesn't snuff it on the spot, he'll drop down unconscious straight-off . . .' And so the litany of mayhem and murder would go until even bloodthirsty Indiano would have enough and roll his dark eyes in disgust.

Now, as the staff car began to roll into sight, bouncing and bumping over the uneven surface of the cliff-top, the first of his Catalans came panting and sweating over the edge, already unslinging their rifles as Tiny's voice came from below, with, 'Now then, don't waste time. Time wastes frigging lives . . . Get to it, lads . . . get to it!'

They got to it. Rifles unslung, they doubled forward, crouched low, their breath coming as if through cracked bellows. Five metres . . . ten metres. They flung themselves down as one, as Bren guns opened up to either side of them, the white tracer criss-crossing lethally to their almost immediate front. For the commando gunners were firing live ammunition, and they had suffered casualties due to their slowness before. Still, they couldn't rest. As thundering fireworks started to explode all around them and hoarse-voiced NCOs yelled, 'Keep moving, you bunch o' pregnant penguins . . . keep sodding moving!', they began to crawl under the two-foot high barbed wire, the ground below hosed down previously to a slippery, sticky goo of mud, so that even on the slight slope, they slid and found their packs catching on the cruel barbs just above them as those deadly machine guns kept pounding away so that, as a watching Cusi knew from personal experience, a trainee didn't know whether to try to keep on going or simply collapse in the mud in complete despair and let anything happen even death.

Cusi shook his head and felt for his poor Catalans, who hadn't bargained on this when they had been fetched secretly to London at night and confronted with a smiling Cusi and a table full of bottles of red wine and great heaped plates of *bottifarra*, the Catalan sausage they hadn't tasted these many days. The nice Englishman named Orwell had welcomed them in Spanish, and had then turned them over to Cusi, who had explained in their natives tongue that his arrest had been a cover for a mission that they had been given. He said he couldn't tell them full details of it yet. 'But,' – here he had paused and stared around their good, honest faces, as if he were seeing them for the first time, 'I can say this. We are destined for a long journey if you join me. At the end of it, I hope and pray that what we do will bring some relief to our poor terrorized country.' He had looked very solemn, so much so that they had paused in their drinking and eating to listen to the rest of his words. 'We may die in the attempt, comrades, but we will do so knowing that we have taken our revenge for what the "Frog" has done to our beloved Catalonia.'

Thereafter they had continued to eat and drink, but without their initial enthusiasm at the sight of the splendid feast. Even Indiano had remained silent and sombre.

That had been three months ago now. Since then, they had trained and trained again. There had been no respite. They were not even allowed to the local pub, a run-down sort of place that, according to their instructors, who were allowed to visit it, served only Scotch. Instead, the Englishman Orwell, who they had discovered was a Socialist, and didn't seem a bad sort of fellow, came every week from Edinburgh or Glasgow laden with red wine and whatever Spanish delicacies he could find so that they could have a feast in the NAAFI, instead of the high point of its cuisine – 'bangers and mash' on 'egg and chips'. Then, in his careful Spanish, he would give them the latest news of their homeland gained from his colleagues in the BBC World Service.

But today it wasn't the emaciated civilian in his battered army van who was crossing the cliff top. It was a large Humber staff car driven by one of those pretty Wrens that this Lieutenant Commander Ian Fleming seemed to favour, and Fleming was obviously in a hurry. Not even glancing at the panting, sweating Catalans charging forward with fixed bayonets and roaring their heads off like Tiny and the other instructors had taught them to do, he rolled down the window on his side of the staff car and cried above the chatter of the machine guns, 'Get in, Cusi! I have something urgent to tell you. We're off back to Troop HQ.'

By now Cusi knew Fleming and his moods, and the fact he could not bear to have his orders questioned. He opened the door and got in swiftly. Seconds later, they were bumping back across the cliff top towards Troop HQ, which was a half-ruined, long-abandoned hunting lodge.

The Wren let Fleming out of the car and, despite his apparent great hurry, he waited till she had opened the door for him and saluted; he was, of course, a great stickler for observing the prerequisites of his rank. Then he took Cusi by the arm and hurried him inside the smelly old building, saying as he did so, 'Today I am going to let you into some secrets, Lieutenant Cusi. You must not speak of them to anyone. If you do—' he shrugged and left the rest of his sentence unsaid as the pretty Wren caught up with them, carrying a modern, light-weight gramophone and a single record bearing the neutral label of a BBC recording.

In silence, the two of them waited till she had set it up, saluted yet again and departed, with what Cusi thought was a significant look at her boss. He assumed they had been sleeping with one another on the long wartime trip from London.

Fleming flung a glance at the great oak door to check if it was properly closed before saying in a solemn manner, 'This is most secret, Cusi. Let me say that it is a recording of a secret conversation in Spain—'

Cusi's ears pricked up when he heard the word 'Spain'. Perhaps now he was going to get closer to the reason for their having been brought here; for he had long suspected it was something to do with the country of his birth.

'A conversation between the two most important men in Intelligence in this country and Nazi Germany.'

'*Nazi Germany?*' Cusi queried sharply. 'The enemy?'

Fleming gave one of his horsey laughs. 'Yes, our enemy – and your enemy, too, Cusi. For now we know something that you don't. When you tried to sink the *Deutschland*, one of your would-be victims was the man we are talking about – Vice Admiral Canaris.'

His grin vanished. He lowered his voice. 'This man, Admiral Canaris, is the head of the German *Abwehr*, the German Secret Service, and he is a great friend of General Franco.'

Cusi pulled a face at the mention of the hated dictator, but said nothing.

'This Canaris fellow speaks fluent Spanish, and has worked in Spain since the First World War, when he arranged with the Spaniards to re-fuel German subs operating in the Mediterranean. But although he is an active German nation-alist who hates Reds and the like, he is also a supreme realist.' He paused, as if he were making a decision whether to go on or not and betray the great secret. In the end, he decided he had to, to obtain Cusi's full cooperation. 'Now, although it was frowned upon in some quarters – indeed, the meeting was forbidden by those in authority – our own head of the Intelligence Service, General Menzies, decided to accord with Canaris's wish[*] to meet with the Hun.'

Cusi whistled softly. The thought of the two heads of the enemy intelligence organizations seemed beyond his comprehension.

'Early this month, then, the two met in great secrecy. In a place called Figueres.'

Cusi nodded. 'I know it. It is my own country.' His eyes grew wet.

Fleming didn't seem to hear; he was too concerned with his own story. Besides, he was not a man to be bothered by sentimentality. 'General Menzies being General Menzies, of course, took his own precautions, and he had arrangements made for this recording to be done secretly.' He indicated the gramophone record. 'I am sure that Canaris made similar precautions. No matter.'

Finally Cusi spoke. 'But what has this got to do with me, sir?'

Fleming grunted, 'Patience. Everything will be explained in due course. Imagine, then, the two of them meeting in some shabby, obscure hotel in this Figueres place of theirs,

*Some sources maintain that although Foreign Secretary Anthony Eden warned Menzies he must not meet Canaris, Menzies disobeyed the diplomat and met the German twice in neutral Spain during WWII.

fencing, taking a point here, losing one there.' He warmed to his theme. 'What a splendid scene it would be for some novelist like, say, Somerset Maugham. The juice one could extract from that kind of interplay between two very crafty old men.' Fleming raised his gaze to the dirty ceiling with odd flakes of paint dripping down like snow. 'Yes, a splendid scene . . .'

'I will not hide from you the fact, General,' Canaris said in the careful English which he had learned in a British POW camp at the end of World War One, 'that I am not in agreement with the Führer's current philosophy vis-a-vis Spain.' He looked across at the British spymaster, whose career in Intelligence went back to the First World War, as his did. He was such a grey man, he told himself. His hair, his face, even his suit were all a dull grey as he sat there hunched in his chair, sipping at the cheap Spanish cognac. Indeed, the Englishman could well be already dead, for he said very little, and what he did was muttered in monosyllables. Yet Canaris knew he was listening, even hanging on to his every word, trying to detect falsehoods, prevarications and the like. No, General Menzies was no fool. He wanted to gain as much information as possible and give away as little as he could.

'I tell you frankly, General, the Führer is fully intent on his plan to capture Gibraltar from you – and to do so, he will need Franco's help. There can be no other way if he is to send German troops through the *Caudillo*'s country to attack the Rock.'

As half-asleep as he appeared, Menzies's brain raced at Canaris's disclosure. He knew that the German would undoubtedly tell him more of what Hitler wanted from Franco – that would be information that would come his way in due course this evening. He needed to gain more. He broke his silence with, 'Your Führer obviously wants to deal with the Rock and the way it guards our Empire supply routes in the Med before he marches east against Russia, I suppose.' He took a careful sip of the *Fundador*, as if what he had just said was not that important.

Canaris caught his breath. The cunning old devil of an Englishman had caught him completely off guard with his question. It was the last thing he had expected to be asked. Still, he knew he must answer it if he expected the Englishman to cooperate with his plan. 'Yes, General, that is the case. The Führer must ensure his rear is safeguarded.'

Menzies grunted something, but his grey, ashen face showed no animation at the thought that he had just been told one of Germany's greatest secrets: soon the *Wehrmacht* would march east against Russia and deal with the Bolsheviks, Germany's real enemy, once and for all.

Canaris gave a little sigh and told himself, as he often did, that the English always seemed so naive and unworldly, yet they were as cunning, in reality, as any damned card sharp. He continued. 'It is planned, therefore, that the Führer will meet with Franco yet again. He hates such meetings. But this one is the decisive one. He intends to force Franco into the attack on the Rock with threats and bribes – and substantial military assistance. You wish to know what exactly, General Menzies?' he offered.

Menzies shrugged those skinny, old man's shoulders of his. 'I don't suppose the military side of it is so important, Admiral. An airborne division to land on both sides of the Straits with the Spanish infantry attacking after a heavy German bombing attack . . . Something like that . . .' His voice trailed away to nothing.

In his mind, Canaris was suddenly full of admiration for the English spymaster. The old devil, who looked half dead most of the time, was up to every trick. He had just gotten Hitler's plan to attack east out of him. Now he obviously already knew a great deal about 'Operation Felix', the attack on the Rock. Menzies obviously had some high-paid informants in the Madrid *Ministerio de Guerra*. But then the 'Horsemen of St George*' had always been used by the English – and they had plenty of them – to buy the information they needed. 'Yes, exactly,' Canaris conceded, knowing that he had met his master in double-dealing and that it was no use trying to fool the

* ie sovereigns, bearing the emblem of St George slaying the dragon.

man opposite him. 'Now, I shall tell you why I am now against "Operation Felix" and Spain's involvement in it. I know and love this country. If God so wills and I survive the war, I shall retire here and toast my old bones in Spain's hot sun.' He smiled.

Menzies didn't return his smile. His face seemed as grey and sombre as ever.

Canaris shrugged slightly and continued. 'Operation Felix would ruin Spain. She has recovered from the last civil war. There are plenty of those Red swine left in the country who would take the opportunity of another war, this time on Germany's side, and the resultant losses and shortages to start yet another uprising. That is something I do not want to see happening, even if I do my own country a disservice in doing so.'

Surprisingly enough, General Menzies nodded his grey head and said, 'I agree with you, Admiral Canaris. We want no more trouble with the Reds here, or elsewhere for that matter.'

Canaris smiled, pleased. Now he could see that the grey Englishman's heart lay in the right place: on the side of the anti-Reds. He continued with more enthusiasm, believing he had gained the confidence of the man opposite. 'Now, my dear General, I am going to confide in you a great state secret, one that is known only to a handful of top people here in Spain and in Germany. It would mean my head, General, if it ever came out that I have revealed it to you, or anyone else for that matter.' He paused and added, 'You understand, of course.'

'I do, Admiral . . . and you have my word that I shall not reveal what you are to tell me to anyone. Please carry on.' There was a firmness in the Englishman's voice, even an eagerness, that made Canaris wonder momentarily whether he should reveal what he was about to. After all, his words could change the whole balance of power in the Iberian Peninsula, even in the whole of the Mediterranean area. But at the same time he knew he *had* to tell the English spymaster if anything was to be done to save Spain. He took a deep breath and commenced.

'Within the next month, General Franco is to meet the Führer secretly on the border here between France and Spain . . .'

Two

Now, with the half-ruin of hunting lodge-cum-commando headquarters blacked out, Fleming had placed a sergeant-instructor on guard at each door. Under the command of the Shanghai Police giant Tiny, they had been ordered by the arrogant naval intelligence officer to shoot without challenge anyone approaching the place. For as Fleming explained, 'Naval Intelligence has declared this whole area within a radius of five square miles out of bounds. We have a battalion of Marines checking the whole area – and we have the authority of Prime Minister Churchill himself to take the most stringent measures against any intruder.'

Tiny was not particularly impressed; he never was. He thought Fleming, as he said to his cronies of the sergeants' mess, 'a proper shit – a typical toffee-nosed twit.' All the same, the fact that Churchill had concerned himself with whatever was going on up here in remotest Scotland did impress him a little. He had told his NCOs as soon as it had grown dark, 'Keep on yer toes, lads. There's something big going on.'

There was. Even a still-puzzled Cusi knew that, as he was ushered into what had once been the big oak-panelled dining hall of the old hunting lodge. He was surprised to find it was full of high-ranking officers from all three services, plus a half a dozen civilians in dark suits and striped pants, who looked and acted as if they were very important, which he supposed they were. All were drinking fine Scotch and smoking expensive cigars or hand-rolled cigarettes while Fleming's Wren driver manoeuvred herself between them carrying sandwiches.

Fleming was naturally in his element. A lot of the strangers present he seemed to know already, addressing them with those strange nicknames that the English, or so it seemed to Cusi, were greatly fond of, 'Bimbo', 'Jumbo' and the like. As for the others he didn't know, he fawned on them, making a fuss over their titles and rank, waving urgently at his Wren mistress or one of the commando instructors, clad in an immaculate white jacket, their shoulder muscles bulging through the thin fabric as if they might split it at any moment.

Cusi sniffed with distaste. He had seen similar crowds in Madrid before the war had started, living in a fool's paradise, believing that nothing could happen to them because of their importance, not knowing that they, too, would soon experience the horrors to come just like the humble, downtrodden man in the street.

'Hola.' He turned, startled, as a voice added, 'Cosy little bunch, aren't they, Cusi.'

It was the scruffy, sick-looking Mr Orwell, whom he knew now was some sort of a writer who worked for the BBC. As usual, he had a glass of whisky in his nicotine-stained hand and a cheap cigarette glued to the corner of his mouth, which he removed, apparently, only when his skinny body was racked by yet another bout of coughing.

They shook hands in the continental fashion and Orwell said, as if slightly amused, 'The great and good, and even the peasants like us, I see, are going to be let in to the great secret at last.'

'Secret?'

'Yes, you don't think that Commander Fleming over there doing his bum-kissing would be training you like this over the last three months so that you can go and get your heads blown off as P.B.I.?'

'P.B.I.?' he queried once again.

'Yes, Poor Bloody Infantry.' Orwell took a drink of the whisky and started to cough immediately, his liquid-filled, tubercular lungs rattling painfully as he tried to stop coughing. Not anyone in that august, high-ranking company seemed to notice; they were too concerned with their own importance to bother about the afflictions of some shabby, working class scribbler, as they thought Orwell.

Cusi frowned. He thought of asking Orwell sharply what he meant. Then he thought better of it. Orwell was a decent fellow who felt about Spain and Catalonia. Besides he was obviously a dying man. He ought to be left in peace.

'*Gentlemen!*' They turned as one, even the self-important civilians. Obviously they were expecting something important from Fleming who had just broken into their drink-fueled chatter. 'Can I have silence, please, and your attention?' Fleming wasn't really asking. With all the assurance of a well-born and rich old Etonian when he spoke, he expected to be listened to, even by these high-ranking people.

Orwell finished coughing, his face flushed an unhealthy red, and winked for some reason at Cusi, who had never quite understood the English habit of winking; Catalans didn't wink. All the same, he winked back.

'I should like to show you a film of the man we are dealing with, taken earlier this year. You will see that he has changed a little since he defeated the Reds in Spain back in thirty-nine.' He licked his fingers. The room went dark abruptly, and at the end of the place a projector started to whirr noisily.

Cusi pricked up his ears as the film began to roll and the unknown commentator spoke in Castilian, his voice full of disgusting respect. It was 'Paco' all right, the 'Frog'. But now he seemed much larger and grander, and definitely very much fatter – something that his well-tailored khaki uniform couldn't hide.

Now, Cusi saw, he wore the uniform of a captain-general, a rank traditionally reserved for the king of Spain, and enjoyed the royal privilege of walking beneath a canopy as he approached the waiting microphones.

'*El Jefe del Estado y Generalisimo de los ejercitos Esponales, por la gracia de Dios, Caudillo de Espana y de la Cruzada,*' the unctuous voice of the Spanish commentator oozed, as somewhere at the back of the big dining room another voice translated his words into English: 'Chief of State . . . Highest General of the Spanish Armed Forces . . . by the grace of God, Caudillo of Spain and the Crusade . . .'

Next to Cusi, Orwell whispered, 'Oh, my God, isn't it just sickening!'

Now Franco waddled closer to the microphones. Officials ran forward to adjust them, as the military band ceased playing and his mounted Moorish bodyguard fought to control their nervous horses.

The dictator didn't hesitate. 'People of Spain,' he cried, 'Our regime is based on bayonets and blood, not on hypocritical foolish Bolshevik elections. That blood and those bayonets won the country of our beloved Spain for us. But ahead lie new dangers, and if the call comes, we must not be afraid to use those bayonets and shed our brave blood yet once again.'

Franco hesitated a moment, almost as if he were wondering whether he should really say what he was supposed to. Cusi noticed the hesitation, as did the Englishman, Orwell. The latter whispered, as Franco's audience down below the grand steps stopped waving their paper flags as if they, too, suspected something was wrong, 'The frog, as you call him comrade, is up to something. You can almost smell it.'

Cusi nodded his agreement but said nothing. Instead he concentrated on the fat dictator, wondering what he would say next. Finally Franco broke his silence. He raised his finger, as if in warning. 'People of Spain, we *do* want peace, I can assure you of that as your leader. But our world is changing. We cannot remain aside from the great changes that are taking place outside Spain. If nothing else, we owe a debt of blood to allies in Italy and Germany who shed their young blood in our noble cause. It is a debt of honour – and we Spaniards have always honoured such debts above everything else, even our very lives.' Franco wagged his fat forefinger, chin raised high and pugnacious, knowing as he did that his double chin didn't look good on the photographs and newsreels. 'So, my people, I must warn you the time is soon coming when we Spaniards must honour that debt.' Abruptly he clicked to attention and thrust out his right arm in the Fascist salute. '*Viva España!*' Down below the crowd echoed the salutation under the watchful eyes of the *Guardia Civil* with their sub-machine guns and tricorn hats. '*Viva España!*'

The screen went blank suddenly, and at the back of the

hall someone turned the lights higher. The illustrous guests started to sip their drinks, and once more the pretty Wren started to circulate with the tray of canapés.

Fleming waited, and then spoke. 'Gentlemen, I don't think one needs a crystal ball to understand the meaning of that little speech that General Franco gave in Seville two days ago and which we have specially flown over here at some expense.' Fleming made the Continental gesture of counting notes with his thumb and forefinger, a cynical smile on his long, broken-nosed face – he meant bribery, his audience knew. His smile vanished and he continued with, 'It is clear that the dear general with the slimy features is going to throw in his lot with Mussolini and Hitler. That is the debt of honour he mentioned which must be repaid.'

There was a murmur of agreement from his listeners, but Orwell could not see what all this was to do with them and why they had been summoned from London to the far north of Scotland so abruptly.

Fleming enlightened them. 'Gentlemen, you all represent agencies which have direct or indirect connections with Intelligence. You, Sir Peter from the Foreign Office, Professor Masterman and your Twenty Committee,* Group Captain Winterbottom from the SIS . . .' Fleming went round naming the important members of his audience with great panache, and Orwell, who disliked his fellow old-Etonian, could not help but admire the way in which Fleming did so. Then he even blushed as Fleming looked at him and said, 'and Mr George Orwell, the writer from the BBC.'

Orwell told himself one day he'd reckon up with Fleming and his kind, but even as he did so he knew that the Establishment would be about dead by then; the war would see to that. Then there'd be a new kind of left-wing establishment, which probably would be much worse. He sighed, and listened again to what Fleming had to say.

'As you are all associated with mainline Intelligence and will have some part in what is to come, I have been

---

* The Twenty Committee, also known as the 'Double-Cross Committee', was responsible for 'turning' German agents and recruiting double agents, especially working for Germany in the Gibraltar area.

authorized by my own chief, Admiral Godfrey and Group Captain Winterbottom's chief, General Menzies, to advise you of this. When it is all over there will be the wildest rumours circulating. There will be finger-pointing. Accusation after accusation, and then the counter-accusation. It is then that we must close ranks firmly. There will be no official records of what will happen. All orders will be given by word of mouth. There will be no mention in your private diaries and things like that. The deed will be done, and *we* will know about it, of course.' Fleming flashed a look around their alarmed or puzzled faces. 'Unofficially. *Officially* we will know absolutely nothing.'

Again Orwell was surprised by the manner that this junior lieutenant commander could dominate his high-power audience, most of them a decade or two older than he, in such an assured manner.

'Officially we will know nothing about *what*?' a voice protested. It was that of Sir Humphrey, the Foreign Office's representative there that evening. He was obviously feeling the effects of the good single malt whisky he had been drinking ever since he had arrived.

For one instant Fleming hesitated, and there was a sudden heavy hush in the old hall, broken only by the steady tread of the commando guards outside on the gravelled paths. Then Fleming hesitated no longer. He said, 'The assassination of General Franco, Sir Humphrey.'

Some stuttered, 'I say.' A few gasped. The Foreign Office man was indignant. 'I don't know whether you remember, Fleming. But it is only two years ago that my old chief, the Earl of Halifax announced publically at the outbreak of war that it is not the duty of British diplomats to carry out its diplomatic affairs by means of assassination.' He stared up at Fleming, fat face flushed and indignant.

Fleming stared back at him. 'No, I do not remember that statement. Nor do I care about it. The world has changed. Our Prime Minister Mr Churchill doesn't give a damn about such things. Who do you think, sir, has given the final authority for this undertaking? . . . Franco must die so that the British Empire may survive, that is the be-all-and-end-all of it. Gentlemen, this meeting, which never took place, please remember, is ended . . . Lieutenant Cusi, I would like to see you in my quarters tomorrow morning at zero eight hundred hours sharp. We have a lot to talk about.' He turned and stalked away into the shadows without another word.

Ten minutes later a confused Cusi was standing outside in the cold darkness watching the fleet of army and civilian cars taking away the high-powered guests so that they could catch the midnight train from Edinburgh's Waverley Station that would take them back to London. Closeted in a first-class compartment reserved for them, they might reach the capital before most of their Whitehall colleagues realized that they had been absent.

Orwell, it seemed, was in no hurry to go, though he, too, had a first-class carriage reserved for him and it was obvious that Fleming wanted to get rid of him under cover of darkness as he was doing with the rest of his guests. Instead he turned to Cusi, standing next to him and shivering, for he still could not get used to the damp, bone-chilling cold of the island kingdom, and said, speaking Spanish so that no one else who might be listening could understand, 'Angles, my friend, remember this, no one can make you do anything you don't want to do. England is still a democractic country. We have some laws still which protect us from authority, though God knows how long they will last . . .' He shrugged his skinny, tubercular shoulders and left the rest of his sentence unsaid. 'You must understand that.'

Cusi didn't, quite. He understood that tonight he had been given information that was going to change his life, but how exactly that would be was not yet clear. 'How do you mean?'

Orwell hesitated. 'They – Fleming – will ask you to do something. It is obvious. All this secrecy and training in these wilds of nowhere sort of thing. It will be something very dangerous for you personally, I think, and for your people. But you don't have to do it, if you don't want to. *They can't make you—*'

'Oh come on, old boy. Let's be getting you on your way. I've packed a bottle of Scotch and a few sandwiches for you for the train.' It was Fleming, and it was obvious he was running out of patience.

Orwell gave up. He took Cusi's hand and said in a low, sad voice, 'Good luck to you, Lieutenant Cusi.'

Cusi took the hand, and as he took it, he knew that he would never see this dying writer again. Whatever Orwell was warning him against, he didn't know exactly. But somehow at that moment he realized that his fate was already sealed. There would be no going back now. Fate would do with him whatever it wished. He started to walk to his quarters in the spectral silver light of the sickle moon. In the car, Orwell, feeling wretched and impotent, opened the Scotch and took a hearty swig straight from the bottle. He had done what he could, he told himself, and even as he started to cough yet once more, he took another drink. It seemed the only way out.

Three

Since that strange meeting of the Whitehall big shots in the run-down Scottish shooting lodge, things had changed dramatically for Cusi and his Catalan volunteers. Two days after the big shots had disappeared, they were ordered to pack what they had in the way of kit, and just as the Whitehall people were, they had been sent southwards under the cover of darkness, only in their case they had been transported in three-ton lorries and not in plush first-class carriages.

The journey had seemed interminable, and there had been no stopping, although the country roads they had taken were blacked out and virtually empty of traffic save for a few military cars. They had not even been allowed to stop to relieve themselves. Instead, they had been forced to balance dangerously on the tailgate, holding on the best they could to urinate, or had urinated through oil funnels squeezed between the canvas hood and the lorry's side.

They had arrived in what looked like a ruined barracks, guarded, surprisingly, by a handful of Redcaps, and informed by Tiny, who had now been transformed into a sergeant-major, that they were in some place called Lincolnshire, and were to be quartered in an old barracks which had once housed a battalion of the local 'Yellowbellies', whatever the Yellowbellies were.

Here they spent three days in miserable quarters, though with splendid meals by British Army standards: *two* eggs and bacon for breakfast, real meat and potatoes for dinner instead of the usual 'tinned cow' and dehydrated potatoes, and in the evening, as much beer as they could drink in the NAFFI – *for free!*

But their days were spent in hard drill on the old Victorian square, learning the precise movements of the British Army's three-hundred-year-old drill ritual – slow march, quick march, presenting arms to mythical officers of all ranks – hour after hour of it till they sweated hard and their bones and feet ached with the constant stamping and Sergeant Major Tiny chasing them up and down the square like some mad shepherd dog, bellowing and cursing at them, shrieking at them to 'swing them arms' . . . 'bags o' swank now, remember who yer are', and 'open them legs, you idle men . . . If anything precious falls out, your dear Sergeant Major'll pick it up fer yer, you bunch o' frigging nancy boys . . .'

Cusi started to feel (for he had to join in the drill parades too) they were trained to join the Brigade of Guards, the first Catalans to do so.

After the Yellowbelly's barracks in rural Lincolnshire, they were again ordered to pack their kit suddenly and be ready to move out immediately after blackout. This time they continued their journey southwards in an ordinary passenger train, packed with soldiers and civilians. The long, slow blacked-out train heavy with the smell of stale human sweat, children's urine and cheap tobacco smoke, was so full that people slept on the baggage netting and in the lavatories, and had to be woken up when babies or little children had to 'go', with the embarrassed young soldiers undoing wet nappies and holding the squawking infants over the pan. The Catalans arrived dirty and sweaty and totally worn out. But there were no cleansing showers or quick naps for them. Instead, they were ordered into a great hangar-like Army clothing store, where Tiny ordered them to strip, although the place was manned by ATS – 'Don't, worry, lads. These ladies have seen more than you have to offer. But don't ask 'em to measure your inner leg, if yer don't want yer handsome faces slapping.' And the khaki-clad women soldiers had laughed uproariously, though they must have heard the same old comments here in this great echoing hangar many times before.

So they had undressed down to their drooping 'drawers, cellular, soldiers, for the use of' and allowed the women soldiers to run their tape measures over their nearly naked bodies to measure them up for what Tiny called the 'Bond Street of khaki battle dress'.

An hour later they emerged from the great hangar, dressed in smart Canadian battle dress which really fitted, unlike the shapeless rough uniform issued to the average British soldier, the title 'Marine Commando' in red stitched neatly to the shoulders. For as Tiny now informed them, as he twirled his newly acquired sergeant-major's pacing stick, 'Now, gentlemen, you can be proud that you are now members of Commandor Fleming's own private commando, Number Thirty, reserved for special operations behind enemy lines.' He lowered his voice and winked knowingly at them. 'At least you'll tell anybody that who starts asking awkward questions. *Si?*' he added in one of the two words of Spanish that he had learned with the Catalans – the other was '*cerveza*' – beer. 'And remember, lads, I didn't train yer to get yer silly bleeding stupid Catalan heads blown off.' There was sudden warmth in the ex-policeman's voice, and Cusi, listening and translating when necessary, saw that Tiny, as tough and imposing as he looked, had taken a liking to the little bunch of Catalan exiles. 'It's a dopey soldier who gets his head blown off. Any fool can get his head blown off. It's the smart squaddie who knows how to keep it in its proper place.' He straightened up to his full impressive height, clasped his pacing stick beneath his right arm and marched smartly up to Cusi and swung him a tremendous salute. At the top of his voice, he called, 'Sir, permission to match the men off, *sir*!'

Awed and not a little frightened by that majestic presence saluting *him*, Cusi stuttered, 'Permission granted, Sergeant Major.'

Three hours later they marched through the gates of the Royal Marine Barracks in Portsmouth, dressed in their brand-new Canadian battle dress, sweating and swinging their arms like veterans, with Tiny standing at attention outside the guardroom, bellowing furiously so that new Marine recruits fled back to their barracks in fear, 'Swing them arms, will you there! . . . Bags o'swank! Left . . . right . . . left . . .

right! Come on now, you bunch o'tarts . . . show these real Marines how to march . . .'

But Cusi, as he watched his men file, faces determined but glazed with sweat, was no longer listening to Tiny's thunderous urging; his mind was on something else. They had reached the end of the road in this waterfront naval barracks. This was the end of the time they had spent in England since the summer of 1940. Now, he knew with the total certainty of a vision, the real war was about to begin again for him and his brave Catalan exiles.

Angles Cusi was right. At eight o'clock next morning immediately after yet another excellent meal – 'the condemned man ate a hearty breakfast,' as Indiano commented cynically, spearing yet another fried egg with his fork, causing Jordi to cross himself hastily – eaten in a separate mess, attended by silent Wrens in white overalls and headscarves, Fleming started his briefing.

He launched into it immediately without any preliminaries, save the warning, 'Any of you chaps who repeats what he hears in here will be charged immediately and sent to the military prison at Aldershot,' and even the Catalans had heard of the dreaded 'glasshouse' there and took the warning seriously.

'Franco, our sources in Madrid tell us, will leave the capital and head for the port of Valencia in the next two weeks. According to our sources, it is his intention to show himself in those anti-Franco areas which fought to the last against his troops.'

He let the information sink in, and Cusi started yet once again to sense that feeling of unease which he had felt as they had entered the gates of the Marine barracks.

'At Valencia, after the usual propaganda show – meeting the Archbishop and the local regional big shots – Franco will board his new yacht, the *Azor*. In it, he will sail along the coast northwards, showing himself at various ports locally, but not landing. That's the reason for his travelling by yacht. It offers much better security than does land travel.' Fleming allowed himself one of his cynical half-smiles. 'No doubt he'll have half the Spanish fleet covering the *Azor*. When

149

he reaches Barcelona, he will land, under heavy army and Guardia Civil protection. There he will attend high mass in the Cathedral, meet members of his Falange Party and veterans of the Civil War – naturally the ones who fought on his side. The others, as you know, are either dead, in exile or in prison.'

His remark met with no response from his listeners, who were part of that crowd, who had been dispossessed, shot or thrown into the Falange *carcel* to suffer starvation and daily beatings, even torture.

Fleming sensed he had made a mistake with his reference, and continued hastily with, 'In Barcelona after the shindig, it will be announced that Franco has completed his official visits and is – naturally – happy to see that a united Spain has given him its full support. Now the self-proclaimed *Jefe del Estado* and *Generalissimo de los Ejércitos Españoles* deserves a rest.'

Cusi knew that Fleming was vain in everything, and was especially so in regard to the foreign languages he boasted to know, but his Spanish was terrible; it grated even on the Catalans, who hoped they would never hear Castilian ever again. He sighed, but listened intently as Fleming concluded his account of Franco's intended journey, relayed by some obscure mole, paid and bribed by Professor Masterman's 'Double Cross' Committee no doubt.

'Franco, according to our sources, would then sail further north almost to the French frontier to land at a little place called Roses, where he would land and journey to nearby Perelada, where he had a summer house – presumably stolen since the Civil War.'

'*Roses!*' Cusi's heart leapt at the mention of the well-remembered name. Immediately it raised memories of the past in his homeland that were not marred by sadness or anger. There in the little fishing village some forty kilometres from the French frontier he had spent the happiest days of his boyhood. When the heat in Barcelona had been unbearable in July each year, his father had closed his *Abogado* practice and had journeyed with his wife and child and Conchita, their servant, plus a caseful of books, which he never read, to the run-down hired villa just beyond the place's *barrio maritimo*, the fishermen's quarter, inhabited, as Father always explained when they drove by again at the beginning of their annual stay, 'by good Catalans, who had had the misfortunate to become Communists', whatever that was. At all events, it was the only place in the fishing village and port to be avoided.

There as a boy, going barefoot as most of the local boys did, he wandered anywhere and everywhere just as he wished. Even Conchita, who always worried about him in Barcelona, constantly warning against the gypsies who were determined to kidnap him, let him have his head in Roses, where everyone spoke their language and one never heard a word of Castilian for a whole month. Here he swam off the little pier, went for afternoon chocolate at the 'English Tea-Salon', a name which always caused his English mother to double up with laughter and maintain, 'I've never seen such a place in England, my Angel . . . The English ladies take their tea quietly and very weak. Not with a brass band playing bull-fight music on the wireless and rough men knocking back strong waters!' And she would smile at him in that loving way that would bring tears to his eyes even now when he thought about his murdered mother.

Now, here in this spartan barrack room with the Victorian red tiles running up the walls below the battered British flags of half a century before, he heard the name of that once well-loved place again and knew that this time, that now in 1941, it was not going to be the site of pleasure that it had been in his carefree boyhood. This time, he was sure, bad things were going to happen there.

Fleming's next words were as sombre as his thoughts were now. 'At Roses, Franco will have other things on his mind than journeying to the cool air of Perelada to spend a quiet vacation among the vines and wine-growers, men. Our sources tell us that detailed plans have already been made to smuggle him from the yacht to the small railway station at Figueres. From there a special train – an express, it is thought, and armoured to boot. Franco is taking no chances with being assassinated in Catalonia. Well, the special train is to take him to the French frontier at speed. There, men, with the agreement of that traitor Marshal Petain of the French Vichy Government*, he will meet the Führer Adolf Hitler.'

Fleming paused and waited for the expected expression of shock. It came, and Indiano shook his fist at no one in particular, exclaiming, 'Those filthy French pigs! Is there no end to their treachery? They always complain they are betrayed. But it is the Frogs themselves who do the betraying—'

'All right, Indiano!' Cusi cut off his outraged statement sharply. 'We all know what the French are. Let Commander Fleming get on with his exposé. We need to know where we come in.'

There was a murmur of agreement from the others, and Fleming gave a careful smile of triumph. At last he had gotten some sort of reaction from these damned wooden-headed Catalan peasants.

'I shall tell you where you come in in a moment,' he said quickly. 'First I must say that, with the agreement of Mr Churchill himself, General Franco must never meet Hitler. Everyone at the top in this government is agreed on that. For we know from Admiral Canaris – you know, Cusi?'

Cusi nodded, but didn't comment.

'That this time, unlike at their meeting last year, Franco will give in to Hitler's wishes. In return for massive German assistance in the capture of the Rock and its return to Spain after two hundred-odd years, Franco will go to war with this country. In short, as I think most of you understand by now, Franco must die.' Fleming spread out his arms in a melodramatic gesture, as if he were a bad actor at the end of an even worse play signifying personal victory.

'And we will play some important part in that assassination?' Cusi said baldly, no emotion in his voice

Fleming frowned and dropped his arms slowly, his moment of triumph spoiled. 'Yes,' he said. 'You will.'

'How?' Again there was no emotion in Cusi's voice.

---

* With German approval, Marshal Petain, with Admiral Darlan as his deputy, had formed a government at the town of Vichy to rule that part of France unoccupied by the German victors.

152

'You will kill him – with the help of ourselves. All available resources will be at your disposal—'

Cusi cut in sharply with, '*Where?*' He didn't want to listen to any more of what Tiny would have called crudely 'Fleming's bloody bullshit'.

For some reason Fleming hesitated.

Outside they were drilling the 'awkward squad', a bunch of young Marine recruits who seemingly didn't know their left arm from their right. A patient drill instructor was saying, 'Now, each of you pregnant penguins is going to tie his snot-rag to his left upper arm. That way he'll know which his left arm is. And what does that mean, Marine Recruit Blair?' A woeful voice replied. 'Don't know, Sarge.' 'I'll tell you, then. It means that your other arm that hasn't got the snot-rag attached to it is yer frigging right arm. Got that, Blair? Left one – handkerchief. No handkerchief – right arm. Now then, steady in the ranks. On my word of command – and please get it right this frigging time – forward – MARCH! . . . By the left now . . .'

Finally Fleming answered Cusi's question; and now his voice was without its usual upper-class Etonian drawl. Instead, it was just as devoid of emotion as Cusi's had been. It was as if Fleming, who so far in this war had been accustomed to sending other men to their deaths without too much thought, had abruptly realized what he was doing. 'You will assassinate General Franco before he leaves Roses . . .'

153

BOOK FIVE

Murder!

One

Things happened quickly after that briefing with Commander Fleming. Overnight they left the Royal Marines' barracks at Portsmouth, saluted, despite the lateness of the hour, by that gigantic ex-Shanghai policeman, Tiny. Standing there in the glowing darkness – further inland they were bombing the surburbs once again – tears pouring down his tough, craggy face, he called as they marched past, 'Good luck, lads . . . remember, a swift kick in the goolies – and then run like hell . . . Good luck, lads.' And they were through the gate, past the surprised sentries and on their way. They would never see England again.

They arrived in Hampshire in the early hours of the morning. As was usual these days, they were treated to a splendid breakfast, with real bean coffee this particular dawn instead of the terrible English tea. Weapons were issued: five snipers' rifles, complete with high-grade telescopes to be used by the Catalans' best shots, plus the new Sten gun for the rest of them. As the RAF weapons sergeant explained, 'You can break it up in three parts, chaps, magazine, butt and cylinder, and hide it about yer person.' He grinned cynically. 'Mind you, it only costs seven and a tanner to make, and I can't guarantee it'll work when yer put the frigger together again.'

Half an hour later they were in a converted Wellington bomber on the long and dangerous flight to Malta, the first leg of their journey. Of Fleming they heard nothing, save a laconic message to Cusi. It read, 'Keep an eye on them. In Malta entertainment to be provided. But don't let them out of your sight. Fleming.' The message annoyed Cusi. He was sending the Catalans to their possible death. Still he didn't trust them not to desert at the first possible opportunity. But the adventure of the long flight over the Bay of Biscay, dominated by the German *Luftwaffe* stationed in France, made him forget his anger speedily. Twice, the Wellington's co-pilot, a big burly Australian with a mighty upswept bushy moustache, warned them there were German fighters in the surrounding air space. And twice they dodged the ME-109's without a shot being fired.

Nearly an hour later they had swept safely across the southern coast of France and emerged into the bright blue of the sky above Mediterranean, ploughing steadily eastwards across the sea to Malta.

'Relax, laddies, now,' the Australian said cheerfully. 'It's the Eyeties down below, I *hope*.' He made a gesture as if he were crossing himself, and Jordi, the Holy Man, frowned. 'They'll be too busy chasing French skirt and getting pissed to worry about us.' He gave them his big toothy smile and handed over the big thermos of hot coffee to Indiano. 'Help yourselves, boys. I've laced it well with grog.' Sitting there in the hard seat, enjoying the blue of a Mediterranean sky after so long away from his homeland, Cusi found himself coughing throatily after the first sip of the unknown mix. But as time passed leadenly, even the Mediterranean paled, and Cusi found himself nodding off, lulled into sleep by the steady drone of the motors carrying the former bomber ever eastwards.

He awoke with a start. The bright sunshine over the glittering sea below had vanished. The cabin seemed suddenly cold, and there was the stink of burned explosive. For a moment, Cusi couldn't comprehend where he was and what was happening. The clatter of cannon fire told him the very next moment. In the middle of the aisle, the big Australian began to crumple, mouth opened stupidly. His eyes filled with tears of pain. Now a stupified Cusi could see he was really only a boy behind that great bushy moustache. The next instant he fell full length in the aisle, and someone yelled in Catalan, 'We're being attacked!' They were, and their attackers bore the black-and-white Maltese cross of the German *Luftwaffe*, and they were coming in for the kill.

Above them and in the tail, the two RAF sergeant gunners took up the challenge, spraying the air between them and the two Messerschmitts coming in from port and starboard, jettisoning their fuel tanks as they did so for extra speed.

Cusi pressed his nose closer to the perspex of the port-hole as the German fighter pilots, roaring in at four hundred kilometres an hour, swung from side to side to avoid the incoming enemy fire. He knew little about aerial warfare, but he guessed that the unknown Germans had to be experienced pilots. They were not going to be put off by the two RAF air gunners. He held his breath and wondered how the pilot was going to escape. Next moment he ducked, as yet another salvo of 20mm cannon shells ripped the length of the Wellington's fuselage.

The RAF pilot reacted immediately. He, too, had to be a veteran. Suddenly, frighteningly, the Wellington dropped out of the sky like a stone. Next moment the two Messerschmitts soared over the plane purposelessly, the cannon shells hissing into the distance without result.

Now Cusi realized what the Wellington pilot was up to. He was heading for the sea far below. There there were wisps of low cloud, in which, if he were very lucky, the Wellington could hide. He'd play hide-and-seek with the enemy fighters till they started to run out of fuel and would be forced to return to their bases in Sicily. Cusi said a quick prayer that he'd pull it off. Otherwise – but he dared not think that particularly dreadful thought to its logical end.

Now all was nervous, yet controlled, confusion. As the Wellington dropped lower and lower, and their two attackers curved round in a great black-tailed circle and prepared to take up the chase once more, Cusi tried to attend to the Australian. But it was no use: he was dead already. 'Revs', the flight engineer, stepped over him, laden with great gleaming belts of cartridges, trying to keep up with the 'tail-end Charlie', who was using up his ammunition rapidly and was preparing now to take up the challenge once more as the fighters came in for the kill. Desperately, up front the pilot squeezed every last bit of speed out of the damaged ex-bomber in his efforts to get down to sea-level before the

Messerschmitts attacked. Cusi, feeling useless and impotent, dug his nails into the palms of his hands willing him to succeed.

The first of the German pilots had obviously lined up the Wellington in his sights. Now he raised his planes evil, yellow-painted nose and at the same time lowered its flaps. Thus he hoped to reduce his speed and provide a sound gun base for some deflection shooting. It was the opportunity that the 'tail-end Charlie' had been waiting for. He seized it eagerly. He opened up his massed Browning machine guns. He couldn't miss such a target. The mass of white tracer slammed into the Messerschmitt. Cusi caught one last glimpse of the suddenly terrified German pilot's face before it disappeared behind a mass of smashed perspex. With a great roar, the Messerschmitt exploded. A black lump came hurtling to the diving Wellington. For an instant Cusi was puzzled. What was it? The next moment he knew. It was the body of the pilot. His knees tucked into his stomach, revolving like a high board show diver doing a somersault, he came so close that Cusi could see a piece of white paper streaming from the pocket of his black leather jacket, behind that trailed the straps of his shattered parachute. A moment later the pilot was followed by another small object revolving frantically as it raced as if in an attempt to catch up with the body of the dead pilot. It was his severed head . . .

They landed just under an hour later at Malta, covered by the airfield's anti-aircraft guns, for the Germans and the Italians were raiding the key Mediterranean island fortress day and night now. Italiano and Jordi helped the pilot from the control. He was ashen-faced, and they had to lever his white-knuckled hands from the controls, using all their force. But as they lowered him to the ground and prepared to drag out the body of the dead pilot, a hard, officious voice snapped, 'Leave the stiff to us . . . Get yourselves into the caves at once. No messing now!'

Even before they knew it, the Catalans and Cusi were running for the island's nearest caves, which acted as air raid shelters for the military and Malta's civilians, and the Wellington was being wheeled to the nearest bomb-bay shelter.

To the sweating, panting Catalans' surprise, the cave they were allotted to by another flustered, even (or so it seemed) embarrassed soldier, was filled with women. But these were not the usual island women: old crones with sun-wrinkled faces, wrapped in black woollen shawls, busy with their knitting and other handicrafts.

These were bold-eyed young women in their prime, their bosoms exposed by low-cut blouses, full of chatter and animated gestures; their nails were painted red, too, as if dipped in blood – and they weren't knitting. Instead they were drinking heavy red wine by the tumbler.

'*Mierda*,' Italiano gasped, mouth dropping open in awe as the young women started to beckon to the new arrivals.

In England a few of them had been allowed to consort with local prostitutes, But they had mostly been old enough to be their mothers. These were flashy, fleshy, vibrant women, full of fire and promise, and now, from the way they were encouraging his surprised Catalans, a worried Cusi was sure it wouldn't be long before they would be putting their promise into direct action – and he was sure that it wouldn't be something that the somewhat puritanical English would approve of.

He need not have worried, for at that moment, a curly-haired officer, a big grin on his sunburned face, popped up his head from the back of the cave (later Cusi dared not ask what he had been doing down there, and the young gunner wasn't volunteering the information) and shouted above the excited chatter of the whores, 'I say, old chap, don't hesitate. It's on the house. Your Lieutenant-Commander Fleming has ordered that your boys should enjoy a bit of the other while you're our guests here on the George Cross Island*. But mind you,' he added, 'you won't get a medal for it, what?'

Cusi didn't know what a 'bit of the other' meant, but he could guess. His men needed not be told either. Their recent brush with death already forgotten in the manner of young men, they were advancing, grinning from ear to ear on the

---

* King George VI honoured the whole of Malta with the George Cross in World War Two.

waiting whores like men who had just seen the gates to paradise open.

Cusi gave a little groan as the curly-headed officer disappeared into the back of the cave once more and the great orgy commenced, leaving him standing there like a fool, feeling the same almost forgotten urges as his men, but not wanting to lose his newly achieved dignity as a British Army officer. But Cusi was not given a chance to succumb to his urges, or to stand back on his dignity. A moment later the sacking curtain that covered the entrance to this smaller cave, filled with half-naked bodies that were already beginning to rise and fall and writhe in sweating passion as the paid-for coupling commenced, was thrust smartly to one side.

Cusi turned, startled. A petty officer in the thick woollen jersey of the submarine service stood there, looking at the scene with a sort of detached envy on his rugged face. He snapped to attention when he saw the single pip on Cusi's shoulder. 'Second-Lieutenant Cusi, sir?'

'Yes.'

'Commander Jewell's compliments, sir. He'd like you to accompany me down to the docks to meet him on the *Seraph*.*'

'*Seraph*?' Cusi queried, puzzled.

'Yessir.' The rugged-faced petty officer took his eyes off Indiano's naked rump going up and down rapidly, 'like a frigging fiddler's elbow', as he told himself enviously. 'His Majesty's Submarine *Seraph*, sir . . .He said he'd like you to come straight away. We're going to have a half hour break in the raids, and he wants to stand the crew down. Got a gharri waiting for us outside.'

Cusi took a last look at his men and shook his head in mock wonder. Even Jordi was leaning back against the damp rock wall with a dangling-breasted whore doing something to him, he had obviously forgotten his religious scruples. Then, pulling his Marine commando beret tighter on his cropped yellow hair Cusi followed the petty officer out into the bright sunlight to where the waiting Maltese coachman and his weary, skinny-ribbed nag were waiting for them.

* See D. Harding: Operation Torch (Severn House) for further details.

It was clear that the lean grey submarine beneath the camouflaged net had seen plenty of action. There were several large skull-and-crossbones marked on the base of her conning tower, scarred silver with shrapnel, and a broom was positioned next to her mast, indicating she felt she had swept the seas clean on her most recent patrol. The few crew who were now on duty on deck looked tough, experienced sailors too, despite their youth.

Commander Jewell was tall, lean and keen. A man perhaps a couple of years older than he was; Cusi could see all the same that he wouldn't tolerate fools gladly. Still, the submarine commander smiled readily enough as he faced Cusi in the tight confines of his cabins over the usual pink gins and said, 'I hear you're the chap who tried single-handed to sink the *Deutschland* back in early thirty-nine. Pity you didn't finish off the job then. No matter,' he raised his glass in a toast and added, 'hope that this time your mission will be completely successful. It will help our cause a great deal. Without the Rock . . .' he shrugged and left the rest of his sentence unsaid.

Cusi sipped the pink gin, which he knew the British Navy drank as their traditional tipple, and not the rum they always talked about, and said, 'I hope so, too . . . If I knew exactly what the details of that mission were.'

'Well, pin back your ears and I shall tell you. I have Admiral Godfrey's and Fleming's permission to do so.' Cusi felt, by the way that Jewell omitted Fleming's rank, that he didn't altogether take to Fleming. Still, he said nothing, eager to know now what the *Seraph* had to do with the mission.

'Our sub has been detached from the 10th Submarine Flotilla, Cusi, and attached to Intelligence to carry out various tasks they assign to us. At first, I and the chaps didn't like it. Our job, we thought, was to knock out enemy shipping and the like. After all, one third of our shipmates in the submarine service have already lost their lives, killed in action, in this war. We thought our main job was carry on the battle in their memory.' He took another careful sip of his gin. 'Surprisingly enough, we have found these Intelligence missions are far more damned dangerous than the routine combat patrol.'

Outside in the terrible, crowded, tight little gangway, some sailor was singing monotously, '*Up came a spider, sat down beside her, whipped his old bazooka out and this is what he said: 'Get hold o' this bash-bash, get hold o' that bash-bash . . . I've got a lovely bunch o' coconuts . . . I've got a luvverly bunch o' balls.*'

Jewell frowned, pulled back the thick curtain that covered the entrance to another private area in the submarine and bellowed, 'Stow it there, Jenkins. Remember, this is not a bloody Welsh choir!'

The singing died away immediately and a Welsh voice said, 'Sorry, sir. We Welsh do love to sing, sir.'

Jewell made a muttered comment, and it was not very complimentary to the Welsh and their love of singing; indeed, he seemed to imply that Jenkins and the rest of the Welsh nation should dispose of their tunes in a rather peculiar bodily orifice. Then Jewell forgot Jenkins and said grimly, 'It's going to be tough, Lieutenant Cusi, and I must confess that I don't envy you one bit. But this is the drill . . .'

Two

General Franco felt very pleased with himself. As he rode in his armoured automobile, surrounded on both sides by his Moorish cavalry with their silken cloaks and mounted on their fine white horses, sabres gleaming in the sun which now shone down on the Catalan capital, he told himself that he had solved that overwhelming problem of Hitler and the *Peñón** at last.

Everything seemed to be playing into his hands now. The English were suffering defeat after defeat in North Africa and his spies there were reporting that soon the Egyptians would revolt against British rule. The English would have enough on their hands when the Germans invaded the Rock; and invade in force Hitler must. Already the Führer was moving the bulk of his divisions eastwards ready for the invasion of the Russian Empire. They'd need to clear up their rear in the shape of the Rock and the Mediterranean before that happened. So if he agreed to enter the war on Germany's side as he intended to, he could now blackmail Germany into giving him everything he wanted. He would ask for the restoration of the war-torn Spanish economy with a massive influx of German currency and aid. Yes, his greasy face broke into a smile of self-satisfaction. 1941 would be the year that would go down in Spanish history; it would be the year that he, Francisco Franco, would restore the Rock to Spain after nearly two hundred years of English domination.

For a moment or two, he forgot the near future and concentrated on the present: his followers lining the route to Barcelona's cathedral, while the patrols of the *Guardia Civil*,

---

* El Peñón, the Rock, ie. Gibraltar.

who were everywhere, kept their hard gaze on the native Catalans, their fingers tight on the triggers of the sub-machine guns slung across their chests. He noted, too, the machine guns posted on both sides of the road his cavalcade was taking. Up on the roofs and the windows of the upper floors, their gunners were prepared to open fire at the first sign of trouble from the crowd below. He nodded his approval and told himself he had already taken a few precautions himself.

He waved yet again as a bunch of Falange Youth raised their right arms in salute and started singing, their youthful voices vibrant with enthusiasm. They were the future, not these wretched stubborn Catalans, and the future was his.

Again he went through the plan for the day. First, High Mass in the Cathedral and a diatribe against the use of the Catalan language. 'Spaniards speak Spanish – there is no other language in this country.' Thereafter, there would be an important speech to Spanish Americans. 'For too long, my brothers in blood, we in Spain have been plagued by the Reds and their denial of God. They have raped our nuns and tortured and killed our priests. Thanks to God and the bravery of the true Spaniards, they have been vanquished and those days are gone. But we, here in the Spanish Motherland, and you, our beloved children in America, must be ever vigilant. We, the defenders of the Faith and the true Spain, must be ever on guard. You in South America must give us as much support as you can. We need not only your material assistance and your spiritual support, but, if the case arises . . .' Again in his mind, the cheering crowds vanished for a moment or two as he pondered the phrase which had plagued him and caused a couple of sleepless nights after he had first decided to give the speech which should reveal to anyone perceptive what were his true intentions now that he had realized that it was time to throw in his lot with Hitler's Germany.

'But if the case arises,' he tried again, fat face creased in thought, 'that Spain is embroiled in a new war and the Anglo-Saxons are involved, we hope you so far away, will come to support and ensure that the Anglo-Saxons remain divided on the issue.' He nodded, and told himself he had said enough, but not too much. If and when Anglo-Saxon England entered the war against Spain, he did not want their Anglo-American relationship to bring the Yankees into the war at their side. The threat of an anti-English and anti-American neighbour – Mexico, for example – right on their own border, supported by the rest of Spanish America, might well keep the Yankees neutral.

Well pleased with himself now that he had ironed out that particular problem, he sat back more comfortably in the sedan and waved to the crowd. Out of the corner of his eye, he caught a glimpse of 'Pepe', Captain Fuego of the *Dragones de Alfambra*. As always, the fat officer slumped in his saddle like a sack of potatoes. Any keen observer would have questioned what such an old and overweight officer was doing in the smart Moorish escort all of whom looked as if they had been born in the saddle. Indeed, the Colonel in charge of the Moors had protested that Fuego should not be allowed to ride with his well-trained Arabs on such an important occasion. Franco had overruled the tough, lean Colonel. He had reasons of his own for taking Fuego along with him on this dangerous expedition to these damned stubborn Catalans. He gave a little nod to the sweating cavalryman bumping up and down on his white mare, which looked as if it were suffering too under Fuego's weight, and then comcentrated on the approach to Barcelona's cathedral . . .

The High Mass and the new Archbishop's address to the packed cathedral had been an outstanding success. Even Franco, who rarely showed his true feelings, allowed himself a smile as he shook the Archbishop's hand after receiving the latter's blessing.

In his address, the Archbishop had taken up the theme dear to his own heart. The pernicious influence of the so-called regional languages – damned peasant dialects, he thought them personally – on the cohesion and unity of Spanish life.

The priest, who had been a fighting padre right through the Civil War and had one eye concealed behind a black patch to show for it, was reputed to have been present right through the heroic siege of the hill-fortress of the Alcázar. It was said, too, that the fortress commandant, Colonel Moscardo, had been summoned to the telephone by the rebels besieging the fortress below and told that if he didn't surrender, the Reds would shoot his son. The sixteen-year-old terrified boy pleaded with his father to give up. But Moscardo refused, telling the boy whom he would never see again: 'Then commend your soul to God, shout "*viva España!*" and "*Viva Cristo Rey!*" and die like a hero.' Legend had it that it was the Archbishop of Barcelona, then an army padre, who had encouraged the old Colonel, whose main concern in life had always been football, to answer in that defiant, inspiring manner.

Whether the ex-padre had ever said those words, or indeed if the Reds had ever shot the hostage teenage son, Franco didn't know. All he knew was that the heroic legend had served his cause well in the Civil War, and that the new Archbishop was serving him well now. Face streaming with sweat beneath his mitre, eye gleaming fanatically, he had trounced the Catalans for their defiant, stubborn use of their forbidden 'dialect'. The atmosphere had grown so steamy that the colonel of *Guardia Civil*, who had his men, both in uniform and in civilian clothes, through the packed congregation, had for a while considered whether he should order the service to be broken off and the assembly cleared at once.

But the harangue had ended with a few subdued boos and a little fist-shaking, which had resulted in immediate arrests so that the Catalan nationalists would realize that any real protest would result in a severe beating, perhaps even worse.

Now, as he passed gravely from the Archbishop's entourage, with the incense flooding outside into the bright afternoon sunshine and the organ playing a Bach cantata, Franco told himself that all had gone well. Now he would be driven back to the *Azul* and enjoy a well-earned rest. Perhaps he would play a few games of cards with fat Fuego, whom he had known as a cadet back in the Infantry Academy in Toledo. At all events, he'd get the too-tight uniform with

168

its stiff collar off and seat himself in front of a cold-air fan. The heat in the Cathedral had been stifling.

As Franco shielded his eyes against the sudden glare of the sun, shining abruptly through the line of dusty trees which fringed the approach to the Cathedral, he was just in time to catch the glimpse of steel. A mere ten metres away, a big man had barged his way through the Falangists waving their paper flags, a knife raised high, heading straight for Franco.

A Moor's steed reared up on its hindlegs, snorting, startled and fearful. For such a heavy man, Fuego reacted quickly. He pulled his sabre from his scabbard and, digging his knees into the sweat-lathered flanks of his big mare, prepared to move forward to block the would-be assassin. But someone beat him to it. It was the tough-looking captain of the *Guardia Civil*. In his haste to pull out his pistol, his lacquered, three-corned hat fell off. He didn't notice. He launched himself at the killer, yelling his head off in the forbidden Catalan tongue. People, screaming and panicking, got in his way. The policeman didn't hesitate. In the same moment that Franco signalled urgently to his old comrade Fuego to remain where he was, the *Guardia Civil* fired. At that range, he couldn't miss. As the people in between fell to the ground, the women covering their ears against the noise, the children screaming, the 9mm bullet struck the Catalan at the back of his head. The back of his skull splintered. Bone, gleaming white like polished ivory against the blood-red mess of his head, flew everywhere. The would-be assassin was propelled from his feet, as if struck by some gigantic fist. He was dead before he slammed to the cobbles, two or three metres away. The *Guardia Civil* captain, however, made sure. Very calmly, ignoring the civilians lying on the ground, weeping and wailing, holding their hands upwards, as if appealing to God Himself to save them, he brought his pistol down. Without appearing to aim, he fired straight at the dead man's face. His features disappeared as if they were red molten wax and dripped onto his skinny chest.

Franco didn't seem to notice. His gaze was on Fuego. He had returned to the ranks of the Moorish escort. He nodded his approval. The procession proceeded on its way. On the steps of the Cathedral, the Archbishop started to rant at the top his voice. Next to him, one of the acolytes began to swing his incense burner wildly from side to side, as if it might well remove the sudden smell of violent death which now hung over the square . . .

Fifty or more sea miles away due east, Commander Jewell of *HMS Seraph* had the Catalans lined up on the slick deck of the little submarine to announce, with Cusi translating, 'Over there to the north are French territorial waters. I don't have to tell you we don't trust the French any more. Only last week, they tried to bomb Gibraltar,' he gave a little self-satisfied smile at the thought, 'and got a bloody nose in the process. We now assume that the French will be allowing Hun subs and destroyers to use their south-western ports. So we must regard these as enemy waters.'

He let his words sink in before continuing with, 'Therefore enjoy the last fresh air you're going to enjoy before we reach the Spanish coast. For a while, we'll proceed below the surface on our diesels. But stuffy, I'm afraid. Most of the time we'll be under silent running. So I suggest, breathe in deeply and enjoy the sea air. Hereafter,' he turned to Cusi and said, 'don't translate this, Lieutenant, it'll stink of unwashed matelots' feet, and if that damned cook serves up sprouts or peas for supper, a good deal of heavy farting.' He smiled wanly, and Cusi smiled back. Jewell was strict, but a 'decent bloke', as the English said.

'What's our expected time of arrival, sir?' Cusi ventured as the Catalans began a dramatic series of heavy breathing, as if their very lives depended upon it, though both Jewell and Cusi knew that at the first opportunity they'd be smoking their heads off, heavy chain smokers that they were.

'We've got to make the Bay of Cadaques – you know it?'

'Yessir.'

'Before dawn. The water there is far too shallow to conceal a sub. So we've got to get there and land you and your chaps while we've got the cover of darkness. Then—' he stopped and looked hard at Cusi, as if he were trying to see something in the Catalan officer's handsome face that only he knew was there, 'it'll be up to you.' He turned and commanded, 'OK, that's enough oxygen. Get below now.'

Obediently, they started to file by him to the conning tower, while Cusi remained behind a few minutes more, and then he followed wordlessly, his mind full of what was to come.

Three

It was two hours before dawn. The normal lighting of *HMS Seraph* had dimmed to a blood-red. The men on duty watch moved quietly, if they moved at all. The rest 'hot-bunked', sleeping in the bunks – if they could sleep – still warm from those who had just vacated them. If they snored, the duty petty officer would go round and press their lips together to stop the noise, for they had all been trained to believe that any noise, however slight, could be heard on the surface.

As the submarine glided ever closer to the tiny, shallow bay, all was tense, controlled silence. At their hydrophones, the operators strained to catch the first sound that might indicate they had been picked up by an enemy. At the periscope, with all eyes on the captain, Jewell, old hand that he was, felt a nerve at the side of his face begin to tick electrically. He understood why; the tension was too great. After all, he was responsible for the lives of three score or so men, Catalan and British.

They crept closer and closer, so slow that they did not seem to be moving. The purr of the diesel engines had been reduced to virtually nothing. In the red gloom, the men's faces gleamed as if greased with Vaseline; they were all sweating profusely. Jewell nodded to his number one, while the Catalans watched open-mouthed. Most of them, as fishermen, had spent their lives at sea. On the surface. Under the sea like this in a submarine was totally new to them. They were fascinated by it, and not a little scared. Jordi, as usual, was praying.

Jewell broke the heavy, tense silence, as he ordered, 'All right, Number One. Up periscope.'

A rush of compressed air. The bright metal tube hushed

upwards. The Catalans jumped. They were taken by surprise. Jewell switched his cap round back-to-front. Swiftly he seized the handles of the periscope. He swung it round in a three hundred and sixty arc. It was standard operating procedure. Nothing to his rear. He turned the apparatus to view the bay. Not a single light broke the inky darkness. Obviously there were no pre-dawn fishermen located here, preparing the carbide lights on the sterns of their craft ready for the dawn's fishing. Jewell offered a silent prayer of thanks. One thing he could do without was a bunch of slow-moving fishing boats. They would really set the cat among the pigeons, now that he was about ready to land the Catalans. 'Down periscope,' he ordered, and as it hissed downwards, commanded further, 'Stop both, Number One. Prepare to disembark troops.'

The throbbing died away. The little grey submarine glided noiselessly now through the water of the entrance to the Bay at Cadaqués. Jewell clattered up the steps inside the conning tower. He opened the hatch. As usual, he cursed as he tried to dodge the incoming sea water – and failed. Below, his number one chuckled, as he always did when the skipper took a splashing.

Carefully Jewell scanned the dark land, with beyond, the faint white of the snow on the mountains. Nothing moved. Not even a dog barked. 'All right, Number One, start bringing them up.'

The younger officer didn't waste time. He knew just how exposed and dangerous their position was in this shallow water, in which it was virtually impossible to dive and remain hidden from observation from above. 'Lieutenant Cusi, take up your first team.'

Cusi didn't hesitate either. He knew the danger. Besides, he was suddenly animated by an almost overwhelming desire to see his homeland again after so much time. He pushed the prow of the canvas sailboat up the inside of the conning tower. Behind him Jordi heaved too. It wasn't hard work. The frail craft which would convey them to shore were made of wood and canvas; still, the Catalans knew they must not damage them in any way. These boats would be their own means of successful escape once it was over.

They reached the top and lowered the boat to the crew on the wet, slippy deck.

Jewell motioned Cusi to stand with him as the other boats followed. Now they and the other Catalans were assembled on the deck, waiting eagerly for the signal to move into the boats. Again, Jewell surveyed the horizon, this time with his night glasses. Still no sign of danger. He decided it was now or never. 'All right, Cusi. I shall rendezvous with you twenty-four hours from now. Remember the signal – two white, one green light. Then move – and move fast. Just in case you're in—'

Cusi realized why the lean young sub commander didn't finish his sentence; he could read Jewell's mind. 'In case they were in trouble.' It was more than likely he would be. Once they had carried out their plan, all hell would be let loose. The whole of this part of Catalonia would be on top-level alert. Every man's hand would be against them, save those Catalans still loyal to the cause. Jewell thrust out his hand. 'Best of luck, Cusi. I – we – are all hoping that every-thing will go off to plan.'

Cusi was moved. Normally the English were so unemotional, but Jewell's words came straight from the heart. He thought fleetingly of all the things that had happened to him since he had been exiled to that cold northern island, in particular of Annabel, even the two military policemen who had arrested him. In the end, they had all meant well. Then he forgot everything save the task in hand. 'Thank you, commander. We'll see you in twenty-four hours.' To his own surprise and that of Jewell, he used that old phrase of his mother: '*Tally-ho!*'

Then he was gone over the side where Jordi was balancing the little boat on the slight swell with all of his old fish-erman's skill. The little fleet, making hardly a sound, started to paddle towards the land.

Jewell watched them, counting off the minutes. He was eager to leave, but he daren't just yet. He didn't want to swamp the boats with his wash. Then he judged it was time to do so. Carefully, thoughtfully, he raised his hand to his battered, tarnished cap, as if in salute, saying to himself,

'Poor buggers.' A minute later the *HMS Seraph* started to pull away gently as the little fleet vanished into the darkness.

Cusi couldn't stop them; perhaps he didn't want to. For he, too, felt a mounting sense of excitement as they drew their craft up along the shingle, looking for a place to hide them for the next twenty-four hours. His men had apparently lost all sense of danger. Some bent and kissed the sand of their homeland, totally carried away by the fact that they were home again after that terrible flight to France in the spring of 1939. Jordi even forgot to pray in his excitement. Instead, he hugged Indiano, the tears streaming down his honest face, babbling over and over again, 'We're home again . . . We're home . . .'

And even that hardened, cynical realist Indiano was moved. Instead of pushing Jordi away, he patted him on the shoulder almost tenderly, like a kind mother comforting a distraught, overexcited child.

Ten minutes later they had concealed the boats beneath the ruins of some farmhand's cottage which had tumbled down the edge of the cliff and formed a rough-and-ready breakwater that would keep the craft from breaking loose and floating out into the bay. Once that was done, they had sunk them below the surface by means of filling them with water and weighing them down with heavy stones. Five minutes after that, strung out in single file as Tiny had taught them, sticking to the side of the hill road, they had ascended the height out of Cadaqués and were heading for Roses, which straggled the coast some two kilometres beyond.

While they marched, weapons at the ready and with Indiano, the most aggressive member of the little band, out in front as their 'recce' (as Tiny had called the advance guard), Cusi ran his mind over Fleming's plan yet once again.

Intelligence, helped by the paid 'moles' in Madrid, had learned that Franco's boat would anchor just off the area covered by the 'English Tea Salon' he remembered from his boyhood and a small restaurant which bore the same name as he himself, 'Cusi'. Here there was a small square where the great man would be welcomed by the *Alcade*, the mayor, who was a Catalan, to be sure, but who had been appointed by the Fascist authorities in Gerona because he had been an early member of the Falange Party. There would be a short ceremony with the Muncipal Band of Figueres, supported by the fife and drums of the town's fire brigade, serenading the dictator while he greeted local worthies, naturally all of them turncoats or members of the Falange. In all, Intelligence estimated the ceremony would last ten to fifteen minutes, including the usual presentation of flowers (naturally in the colours of Spain and the Falange) by the children from the nearest *collegio*. They would, of course, be the children of the local officials.

Security would be taken care of by Franco's own guards from the ship and the Roses part of the *Guardia Civil*, commanded by a Commandante Suarez from Madrid, a notorious sadist and skirt-chaser, given to rum. The only weak point in the security arrangements, as Intelligence saw it, was the fisherman's quarter, the *barrio*, against which Cusi had always been warned as a boy by his parents. It was to be cordoned off by troops from the Figueres. 'All to the good, too,' Fleming had stated when he had first discussed the plan with Cusi. 'The troops are the only ones equipped with radios. Anything going wrong and they would alert the whole area. But we've been told by Madrid that Spanish wireless equipment is hopelessly out of date, and has a range, at the most, of half a kilometre . . . When the balloon goes up, therefore, there'll be nobody on the spot before the Tearoom to alert the whole area. In the confusion, it should give you and your chaps a golden opportunity to do a quick bunk.' He didn't say the words with any conviction, and even then Cusi had been aware that Fleming really didn't give a damn whether they made it back to safety or not. They were expendable, once they 'bumped off' Franco, as he had put it in his usual flippant manner.

They breasted the height. Below lay Roses. To their right lay the ruined medieval castle, built at the time of the Moorish invasions, guarding the entrance to the bay at Cadaqué, and below, the front of the little fishing port. He paused, and let his men get their breath. He walked to where Indiano crouched, surveying the scene, noting that there were some muted sounds coming from the fishermen's *barrio*. Perhaps their womenfolk were preparing the men's breakfast before they went down to their nets and boats. Cusi sniffed. More than likely, from his memories of the left-wing fishermen of Roses, their breakfast would be liquid, and their women would be on their backs enjoying the traditional fishermen's last act of love. Superstitious as all fishermen were, they believed they might not survive the day's venture out to sea, and would enjoy what they called, 'a fuck, the poor man's bread.'

A sound, unidentified for the instant, broke into his fond reverie. Immediately he forgot the fishermen's strange customs. Next to him, Indiano tensed and brought up the little Sten gun, clicking off 'safety' as he did so. Hardly daring to breathe, their nerves jangling, the two of them stared at the hillside beyond the ruined castle. Someone or something was coming down from it, winding in and out of the stone ruins.

'What in hell's name—' Indiano began.

Cusi cut him short with a hushed, 'Sheep or goats. Can't you hear the bells? It's a herd of some kind.'

Now the two of them could hear clearly the musical noise made by goats and sheep which wandered half-wild in the foothills of the Pyrenees; and they knew, too, with a growing sense of alarm, that only rich people owned such animals in a ruined post-Civil War Spain. The shepherd or goatherd might be poor, but his employer would be rich – and in 1941, rich people, deadly scared of the 'Reds' as they still were, supported General Franco.

Indiano pressed his head close to Cusi. 'What we going to do?'

'Hope he passes by and doesn't see us. Those herders are usually half asleep or half drunk most of the time. After all, they're attending to the flock day and night.'

'And if he isn't?'

'We'll worry about that eventuality when it—' Cusi broke off abruptly. An animal was approaching, and he could tell from the lack of smell that went with goat or sheep that it wasn't one of those fearful, harmless creatures. It was a dog, one of those vicious beasts that herders used to protect their flocks – and this one had scented them. It was coming straight for where they crouched, frozen into immobility.

It came closer. Now the two men could see it in the gloom. It was almost slithering along on its belly, nose twitching, its ears back close to its long, ugly skull. It was one of those half-wild dogs bred by herders in the mountains from the local wolves and domestic canines: fearsome creatures with the weight of the domestic sheepdogs and the cunning and ferocity of the wild ones.

It came closer and closer. Cusi felt the cold sweat of fear begin to trickle down the small of his back. Next to him Indiano raised his Sten gun just very slightly. The dog growled in warning. 'Don't shoot,' Cusi whispered. 'You'll have the whole neighbourhood alerted.' He stopped short. He dared not say any more. For the dog was turning its head slowly in his direction, tensing its haunches as if it were ready to spring at any moment. Cusi said a prayer it would go away.

It didn't. Instead, it started to crawl once more, its fur rubbing against the cropped grass. Now he could smell its fetid odour. He felt like retching, but one more sound and the dog would spring. He knew that instinctively. He tried to control his breathing. For a second. Next moment he was breathing hard and loud once more.

The dog came ever closer. The men and the animal were separated by a mere couple of metres now. At any minute, it would act. What were they going to do? Even as he posed the question, Cusi felt the tension break. With an angry snarl, the dog launched itself into space. Cusi acted instinctively. As he was smothered in stinking fur, he grabbed for the animal's genitals. It was his only defence. The dog yelped with pain. It lashed out with its front paw. Cusi stifled a cry of agony at the very last moment as the razor-sharp claw raked his cheek and blood welled up the length of his face. He increased the pressure on the animal's genitals. Madly, furiously, it writhed from side to side, trying to break that hold, lashing out blindly time and time again. Cusi swung his face from side to side, fearful for his eyes.

Suddenly a mesmerized Indiano broke his self-induced trance. Dimly Cusi could hear the steel of his commando knife as Indiano drew it from its sheath. He whipped it out, and in the same instant threw his free arm around the thrashing dog in an attempt to keep it still.

'In the name of God, Indiano,' Cusi sobbed, at the end of his tether, 'kill the bastard – *Quick!*'

The other man didn't hesitate. It was as if he were suddenly seized by a great rage, as if this shouldn't be happening to him. He wrapped his arm round the dog's head. Indiano thrust his two fingers right up and inside the animal's nostrils, hating himself for having to touch such filth, but too angry not to. He bored his fingers ever higher. Blood spurted down them. The dog thrashed its head, but it couldn't break that iron grip. Next moment Indiano jerked the head back with all his strength. With his free hand he thrust his knife into the animal's exposed throat. More blood flooded his hand, hot and disgusting. He didn't let go; he couldn't. With the last of his strength, he drew the razor-sharp blade along the throat. The animal went limp. Cusi hung on with all his strength, not daring yet to relax his grip. The dog quivered mightily. For a moment, the two men thought it was reviving. But the shiver ended in a kind of soft whimpering. Then it was dead, and they lay there like lovers, still holding the dead sheepdog, listening to the approach of its master, calling out the dog's name, coming towards them, not knowing he was coming to his death . . .

Four

Like the old soldiers they both were, Franco and Fuego rose early, as they had done as cadets back in Toledo. But now they were old and had achieved rank, they took their time, as they would have done in some North African officers' mess, when the younger ones had already left to carry out their duties before the African sun struck the eyeballs like a sharp knife, and conscripts faltered and fainted on the white, flaming barracks square within minutes of coming on parade.

Their boat had come to rest now just off Roses, rocking gently on the early morning swell as the barefoot sailors scrubbed the deck and polished the brass before they made their ceremonial entrance to the little harbour in an hour's time. Despite their differences in rank, they chatted easily, made mild jokes at each other's expense and called one another by the familiar '*tú*', a form of address that even Doña Franco never dared use to her husband.

For a while Franco had regaled his old comrade with the details of the British and locally recruited battalions that currently defended the Rock. He reeled them off without reference to notes: 'the King's Regiment, the Somerset Light Infantry, the 4th Black Watch, you know, Fuego, the English who wear skirts like women.' He grinned, and his old comrade said, 'Now I see why you have made general and I am a mere major. You have an eye for detail.' He passed another demi-tasse of bitter black coffee laced with cognac across the breakfast table towards Franco.

Still unshaven, the master of Spain, clad in a loose dressing gown over his underwear and the body belt which he hoped would pull in his belly so that he didn't look as fat as Fuego, who could have been his double in height and flabbiness, shook his head. 'No, my dear friend. Not detail, but luck. You know what the Frenchman Napoleon said: above all he wanted lucky generals. I have been lucky.' He sipped his coffee delicately – for a soldier. 'Now I hope I will be lucky again in my dealings with Herr Hitler and the Fritzes.'

Fuego smiled. He didn't envy Franco his success. The Generalissimo would probably die young of a heart attack or something through worrying about his responsibilities as head of state. He hoped to live till old age, enjoying his cognac and being serviced once a week by some fiery young *gitana* whore.

'So, all in all,' Franco resumed, preparing his figures for the meeting with Herr Hitler, 'the English will have six of their own infantry battalions, plus two local brigades – and they'll fill their pants and run as soon as they see the Germans – and no air force to speak of. One good German airborne division, and our own infantry support from La Linee, and that should put paid to the English, and the Rock will be Spanish again after two centuries of foreign occupation.' He beamed at his comrade and ran his hand across his unshaven face, telling himself he'd soon have to get ready to face the Catalan pigs on the shore.

Fuego beamed back. 'You'll go down in history, General.'

Franco frowned. Sometimes Fuego was too casual, too cynical. One didn't know when he was serious or just making fun. 'I hope, too—' he began, as next to him on the leather seat the phone started to ring urgently. He picked it up and listened, his relaxed mood vanishing visibly.

Fuego waited till he was finished. For a moment or two, Franco simply sat there without speaking. Fuego said, 'Problems?'

'No, Fuego. But we'd better get dressed.'

'The usual uniform?'

'No, Fuego. We'd better be prepared. After all, this is Catalonia,' he said swiftly. 'The four star.'

Fuego frowned, but he didn't ask why he was to wear a full general's uniform this fine summer's morning. He had done so before, and he'd probably do so again before he got too fat to play the double role. He gathered his dressing gown about his flabby body and was gone, leaving Franco alone with his thoughts. They weren't particularly pleasant . . .

From their vantage point in the tower of the village's old church, Cusi and Indiano could survey the whole sea front and little square in front of the English 'Tea Salon', where Franco would land from his brilliant white boat further out in the bay, its brass glittering in the morning sun.

It was a splendid day. The sea was a light blue, and as smooth as a mirror. Not a single cloud marred the perfect sky. Already the locals, dressed in their shabby best, were being ushered into the landing place square by the *Guardia Civil*, most of them armed with sub-machine guns, their officers carrying swords in honour of the great occasion. Behind them in the fishermen's *barrio*, the most likely source of trouble, the conscripts in their sloppy, ill-fitting uniforms had set up 'Spanish riders', mobile barbed-wire barriers across the road from Cadaqués, which were now being covered by machine guns, manned by NCOs of the regular army, all of them, to judge from their medal ribbons, veterans of the Civil War.

Next to Cusi in the shadows of the church tower, Indiano grunted, 'shutting the stable door after the horse has fled, eh?'

Cusi, busy with the problem in hand nodded absently. That was *not* the way they'd take back to the rendezvous point once they had carried out the assassination. They'd head straight inland into the hills, knowing that the only communications, those of the soldiers down at the *barrio*, would have been severed. In the expected confusion and panic after Franco's murder, the authorities would be unable to communicate with one another in Roses, or with the outside world in Figueres and Girona inland. Till they did, the Catalans would have time to escape and lead a false trail that would take their pursuers away from the Bay of Cadaqués.

Down below, the local fife-and-drum corps had broken into a fast march. Cusi frowned. The same Catalans who had once played the solemn, intricate music of the *sardana* now

182

performed to the music of the enemy. He dismissed the turn-coats. Once democracy came back to Spain, they'd be dealt with. Instead, he turned his attention to the boat. Now he could hear the sharp, crisp orders floating across the sea as the boats were lowered, the Spanish flag which he had come to hate hanging limp at their sterns. It was the Franco entourage. The Frog was heading for the shore, and, Cusi told himself with a crooked smile, his last military parade.

Now the two Catalans moved quickly. They had already arranged what they called the 'snipers' nest '8, a pile of old sacking they had found at the back of the church when they had broken in just before dawn. On it, they would rest comfortably, so that nothing would deflect them from achieving a true aim. Settling there with the two telescopic rifles the English had supplied them with, they ejected the gleaming brass cartridges from the breeches one last time. Each man carefully wiped each single bullet that they had oiled earlier on to ensure that they didn't jam at a crucial moment. Then they tested the spring release. The releases worked perfectly. Cusi looked at Indiano. He grinned back, crooked teeth bared like those of a wild animal. He knew he could rely on Indiano. He thought of his dead parents, murdered by the Fascists, and told himself, come what may, he would not deflect from his sacred duty to them. Franco would die.

Below, the music had grown louder. The Figueres munic-ipal brass band had joined in. Naturally it was playing the Falange hymn 'Cara al Sol', with the big drummer already sweating heavily, beating the time as if his very life depended upon it. Indiano raised his rifle and went 'ping'. He grinned. 'End of one fat Fascist pig.'

Cusi grinned and whispered, 'Save your shooting for the real Fascist pig. Here he comes, old friend . . .'

Commandante Suarez looked puzzled. As the Generalissimo puffed his way up the steep, worn, slippery steps that led up to the quayside and the waiting parade, the civilians already waving their paper flags and cheering loudly, '*Viva el Caudillo . . . Viva España,*' his fat, sweating face revealed nothing. It was as haughty as ever. He didn't seem a bit worried by his, Suarez's, report earlier on that something strange was going on; why else the dead dog and the herder with his scraggy throat slit from ear to ear? If he had been one of that fisherman rabble from the Red *barrio*, it would have been different. The Reds were always slicing one another up in their drunken quarrels over catches and the like.

He rubbed the dust off his polished boots with his handkerchief and adjusted his medals. He would stand behind the *Alcade*, not because he respected the fat mayor, but because if anything went wrong – and unperceptive as he was, he felt something might – the mayor could take responsibility, not he. Behind him in the *Guardia Civil*, the phone was ringing urgently. He didn't hear, but luck was on the side of Commandante Suarez. Paco, the one-legged veteran who cooked for the police, did. He started to limp to pick up the phone: a movement that would result in his receiving a medal from the *Caudillo* personally, and more importantly, a new plastic leg that didn't rub so painfully on his stump . . .

The *Caudillo*, panting mightily, bent and, receiving the flowers from the pretty little girl with the Falangist ribbon in her hair, kissed her the best he could, out of breath as he was. Ahead of him the crowd cheered ever more, and the children waved their flags as if they were prepared to shake their skinny arms off. To their right, the guard made up of *Guardia Civil* veterans of the Civil War presented arms, and the kettle-drums of the fife-and-drum band rattled away. All was going to plan, and Commandante Suarez told himself he was being a nervous fool. These Catalan bastards had had the shit knocked out of them. What trouble could they cause? The dead herder and his slaughtered dog must have another explanation. Soon the ceremony would be over, and he could ease off these shitting tight boots and sink an ice-cold beer down his parched throat. There was nothing to worry about.

Handing the flowers to the aides clustered about him officiously, Franco moved towards the rigid ranks of the *Guardia Civil*. Old soldier that he was, his inspection of such formations was not as perfunctory as it would have been with a politician. Franco was very keen, always on the lookout for an undone button, a speck of dirt, a rifle sling not adjusted the right way. In a minute he would reach the flag at the end of the first rank, carried by Corporal Mendoza, the tallest man of the guard of honour, where he would honour the flag of Spain in the true manner of a regular soldier. Franco would pause, salute for what would appear to a sweating Corporal Mendoza a damned eternity, then bow stiffly and pass on his way to the second rank.

Up in the tower, Cusi nudged Indiano. 'Ready, you old rascal . . . When he reaches the flag.'

Indiano, deadly serious now, didn't take his eyes off his front. He grunted something and tucked the brass butt of the British rifle tighter into his right shoulder. Lying next to him, Cusi did the same. He clicked off 'safety' and peered down the sight. Franco had nearly reached the flag now. Gently, he eased his finger round the well-oiled trigger. It moved perfectly, and he felt that old sense of power that he had always felt when handling a weapon, especially a good rifle, in action. In a moment he'd fire, and the next second Indiano would do the same. The tyrant would be dead at last.

He looked at the foresight through the scope, trying to avoid any shadow inside the gleaming glass circle, which would mean he had not sighted the sniper's rifle correctly. Now Franco had turned his back and was preparing to salute the flag. It was time.

Inside the cool entrance to the *Guardia Civil cuartel*, Paco picked up the phone, '*Oigo*,' he said routinely, 'I listen.' He took his toothpick out of his mouth, ready to receive the message. It might be something important; after all, it wasn't every day that someone telephoned the Guardia HQ, especially when the Chief-of-State visited.

It was.

'Urgent . . . ready? *Repeat, Urgent – Ready To Take Message!*'

Paco clicked to attention the best he could with his wooden leg. There was no mistaking the authority in the voice at the other end. He was talking someone important, very important indeed. '*A su servicio, mi colonel*,' he snapped in his best old-soldier manner, making a wild guess that the speaker had to be a colonel at least.

'*Bueno*,' the excited voice at the other end ordered. 'Sound the general alarm at once. Find Commandante Suarez. Order him to stand to in full battle order. Troops on the way from Figueres already. State of emergency, national emergency. Protect *el Caudillo* even with your own life . . .' The unknown officer rapped out the orders like blows from a hammer while Paco's head reeled, realizing that he, an awkward cripple, had, for a moment the life of the Leader in his dirty, work-worn hands . . .

Franco was standing very erect, for such a plump man, white-gloved hand rigid in the salute to the flag. He looked as if he would stand there for ever. It was the ideal opportunity. Cusi knew that he would never get another such as this. 'Now!' he commanded, not taking his eyes off that perfect target for an instant. He took first pressure, trying to control his breathing. Next to him, Indiano did the same eagerly. He was not going to be outdone by Angles. He, too, had a lot to avenge. Cusi took final pressure. The rifle seemed one with his hard shoulder, part of him. He fired.

Franco staggered wildly like some drunk. Through the calibrated, gleaming glass of the scope, Cusi saw how the uniform at the point he had aimed at seemed to jump, split and then eject blood in a bright red fountain that sparkled in the morning sun. The aides appeared petrified, unable to move, hardly believing the evidence of their own eyes. His knees seemed to tremble, about to give way like those of some new-born foal.

Hastily Cusi ejected the smoking cartridge case. Next to him Indiano beat him to it before he could load and fire another round. He gave an atavistic cry that seemed to come from the depth of his being. The impact made the dying leader spin round, his cap slipping, his dark, well-oiled hair, of which he was so inordinately proud, falling over his face foolishly. He was dead before he hit the ground, and the flag of Spain drooped over him . . .

*   *   *

The klaxons started to sound their urgent warning. Abruptly there were armed angry men in uniform running back and forth everywhere. Up at the *barrio* where most of the Catalans were located, there was the sudden chatter of a slow machine gun, followed an instant later by the angry snap and crackle of the fire fight as Cusi's men fought back the soldiers stationed there.

On the upper deck of his boat, Franco lowered his field glasses for a moment and crossed himself solemnly, for he was a pious man who took his observances seriously. 'Thank you, old comrade,' he whispered to himself, as someone spread a cloak over his dead double. 'Thank you.' Then he put on his cap as the skipper of the *Azor* began to carry out his surprising new order, and the boat turned to head out to sea, bound for Valencia. He would not now see Herr Hitler. Dealings with the Germans were too dangerous. That damned British Secret Service of theirs, as he had always known, had their agents everywhere. They had not succeeded this time, but they might the next. Hitler would not attack the Rock this year, and, if he had his way, never would.

Franco was not a fanciful man, but as he looked back at the confusion of the quayside at Roses with the bloody dead stretched out on the cobbles and the bandsmen throwing their instruments into the carts that had brought them there in panic, he realized that he had missed his part in the long history of Spain. He had indeed won the Civil War for the party of the right. But it was a hollow victory. Spain was still divided. When he died, there would be no other strong man of his calibre capable of holding Spain together. It would fall into sectarian and geographic divisions, as it had been in 1936. The only way that he could have really united Spain, whatever the language, the area, the political allegiance, would have been by the conquest of the Rock from the English occupiers. Now that wouldn't be. The Rock would remain under their occupation, and Spain would remain divided. He sighed, thought for a brief moment of the dead Fuego and the need for another double; then he went below to his stateroom to pray and drink, forgetting the whole bloody wearisome business in the manner of the old soldier that he was . . .

* * *

187

Some fifteen or sixteen hours after the *Azor* had departed and a strict curfew had fallen over Roses and, indeed, over all of that part of Catalonia, *HMS Seraph* surfaced with hardly a ripple just off the bay at Cadaqués. While the whole crew stood at alert, with lookouts both to stern and bow, Lieutenant Commander Jewell was poised at the top of the conning tower. Next to him stood his second-in-command, ready to give the signal to dive at a moment's notice.

Jewell peered at the inky darkness to his front. Not a light was visible. It was as if the whole land to his front was empty of humanity. Behind him, out to sea in the Gulf of Leon, he could hear the faint hum of aircraft. Occasionally a flare would light up the far horizon. The noise and the glow told an anxious Jewell that Catalonia was very much alive. They were still searching for his sub and the man who had attempted to kill Franco. He took a deep breath. Next to him, the other young officer tensed. This was it.

Jewell started to work the lamp, flashing the signal that would bring the Catalans under Cusi to the rocky rendezvous at the entrance to the little bay at Cadaqués.

As he wrote a little later in the ship's log* *'0200 hrs reached RZ. Signalled as agreed. Three times. Waited off shore thirty (30) minutes. Enemy aircraft. Returned to the Gulf. As agreed, returned to RZ the next night (21.6.41). No response to my signal. Sent urgent "immediate" signal to Lt. Commander I. Fleming N.I. He replied approx. 0400hrs. Instructed to abandon pick-up attempt. Lt Commander I. Fleming signalled: "Sub more important than Spaniards . . ."'*

---

* Held at National Archive, Kew.

Duncan Harding is Surprised

Rodrigo Nunez, or 'Rod' as he had said I should call him as soon as we met at the airport, probably hadn't written the letter himself – his English wasn't that good – but he knew all about Cusi and the Catalan business all right. He was average height, dark and with keen black eyes. He was casually dressed, but obviously a serious man. After all, in that first letter, he had written, 'Dear Duncan, I have read your books. I know they are not true (?) but parts of them are. For this reason, and the fact you are well-known in England, I would like you to tell the story of the British Secret Service and Generalissimo Franco . . .'

As we walked by the sea, Rod, trotting beside me, said, 'You saw the Lady Tidmus McLeod?' I nodded and took my eyes off the couple of brown-uniformed cops who obviously watched me as a Brit, in case like my 'booze-cruising' countrymen who holidayed in these parts, I pissed or puked or even dared to take off my clothes (that would have frightened the natives, I can assure you) in public. As Rod had explained in his fractured English, 'They arrest you. You go to prison or pay fine . . . especially you Brits'. I nodded. 'And she say?' Rod asked.

We turned towards the *Ramblas*, full of touts handing out leaflets for clubs. It seemed a long way from that nursing home. I shrugged, 'She told me about Lieutenant Cusi, who'd been her lover and the other Catalans, and how Ian Fleming, you know the bloke who wrote the James Bond books . . .'

'He's good, very good. The English are very good with spies, mostly.' Rod's dark eyes flashed, momentarily. 'Anything more?'

'Yes, she said they had all been betrayed that summer of

1940.' I answered baldly, wondering why I'd said the words even before I'd finished them. He paused, catching my arm and holding me from moving further in the Spanish fashion. 'You know, Duncan, in the Generalissimo's time' (there it was again, the 'Generalissimo') 'they shot traitors here in this very square. On the knees, with a bullet to back of the head.'

Now I ask you gentle reader, what are you to say to a statement like that? I didn't know. So I grunted, then waited for the little Spaniard to go on, which he was obviously eager to do.

'Yes, that's what happened to Cusi and the Catalans.' I must have been a bit thick that night, because I said, '*What happened*, Rod?' Rod looked up at me with what old-fashioned writers would have called a knowing smirk on his face. 'They shot them – here in this square. Secret at night. But the bodies were left for people to see. Next morning, you understand?'

I didn't. I said, puzzled, 'As far as I have learned, they disappeared. Nothing was ever heard of Cusi and the others again.' Rod responded immediately; that knowing smirk of his broadened. 'You want a drink, I tell you.' I didn't want a drink. But something told me that if I didn't find out what Rod knew now, I never would, and I needed that final mystery clearing up if I was going to make anything really worthwhile of the book.

We went over to one of the many little cafés of the area, squatted on the wicker chairs, and he ordered 'café negro'. The waiter pulled a face because he didn't order in Catalan. But I'd already noticed ever since I'd met Rod that he'd consistently used Castilian, as if he were going out of his way to show he had nothing to do with the Catalans. '*Bueno*,' he said finally when the waiter had gone, 'It is a mystery, eh. Even your Mr Bond would find it a great mystery.'

I didn't comment. Fleming's Bonds are not my cup of tea. 'Now I shall solve the mystery for you. You have known of "Jordi"?'

'The holy man, as they called him?' I asked, confused.

'Holy? *Si, si*, the holy one. Yes, Jordi was very holy. He

become a monk again before he dies.' I must have looked puzzled at the way the conversation was going, for he said hastily, 'He was the brother of my grandfather. Now you understand, Duncan, you are an intelligent man.'

I didn't really; in fact I was bloody totally puzzled. But I did my best to look intelligent, a mosquito buzzing around viciously, ready to strike a pale-faced Brit the moment he lets his guard down. Stupidly I said, 'You were related to this Jordi?' Then it struck me. *But he didn't die in 1941* if he became a monk later. Crikey, what happened? (And I can assure you, gentle reader, I didn't say 'crikey'.)

He told me. Jordi had indeed got religion again. Secretly he had grown to dislike his fellow Catalans and their ungodliness. In his eyes, the best that Rod could describe it and I could understand, he had come to see them as sinners, who couldn't be allowed to get away with the murder of the 'Generalissimo', who after all was a pious Catholic and the defender of the faith against heathen godliness. Back in Scotland, and later when in training in 1940/41, he had consulted his priest about it, and somehow the latter had put him in touch with the Spanish legation in London. 'You mean,' I interrupted Rod, hardly believing what I was saying, 'the Fascists had known all along what the plan was?'

'*True* Spaniards,' he corrected me earnestly in the same instant that I lowered my guard and the bloody mosquito stung me. 'A Spaniard who should be honoured especially now, when Spain . . .' He stopped. With a look of utter contempt on his dark face, he pointed to the club opposite, where a crowd of young Brits milled about drunkenly, spilling their beer all over the Spanish streets.

Rod needed to say no more. I could understand that bit. Drunken young Brits puking all over the place, older ones buying up the 'sea, sun and sangria', living in their little ghettoes and not speaking to a Spaniard for months on end unless it's a waiter and not knowing a word of Spanish when they do.

'I wish you to tell the story. Not the story of the bad English Secret Service and the Catalans under Cusi, but the story of a true Spaniard like my dead Uncle Jordi . . .' His words trailed away to nothing. Fanatical as he probably was, he could see he'd lost me. He signalled to the waiter; 'La cuenta' he ordered. I was no longer listening. Even an old hack like me has his pride. Cusi and the cruelly betrayed Catalans, even Fleming, had believed in something: they were fighting for a good cause. Perhaps Jordi, the traitor, was too. But that was Ron's problem, not mine.

That old lady in Meadow Field Home for Gentlewomen had said 'It was the summer when we were all betrayed, of course'. Publisher's advance or not. I was not going to betray them again. My publisher would have to forego his 'Rothschild' plonk the next time he went to the 'Gay Hussar', I wasn't going to write his 'celebrated historical work' for him. So I got up and walked away. To the hotel, I suppose. Rod got to his feet but he didn't say anything. Neither did I. I didn't look back. As young as the Spaniard was, he was just as much of the past as were Cusi, the Catalans, Fleming and Orwell. Hacks like me are not much concerned with the past, really. We can't afford it. We have to battle to keep ourselves afloat financially for the future. Winter was approaching, and they say heating costs are going to go up. I shivered at the thought. I'd better start writing something! . . .